Her Unraveling

She will stop at nothing to protect her family.

Luce M. Prince

Copyright © 2023 All rights reserved

No part of this publication may be copied, reproduced in any format, by any means, electronic or otherwise, without prior consent from the copyright owner and publisher of this book.

This is a work of fiction. All characters and happenings in this publication are fictitious and any resemblance to real persons (living or dead), locales or events is purely coincidental.

To my family.

Table of Contents

Chapter 1.. 5

Chapter 2.. 14

Chapter 3.. 22

Chapter 4..35

Chapter 5.. 41

Chapter 6..48

Chapter 7.. 56

Chapter 8..67

Chapter 9.. 74

Chapter 10.. 89

Chapter 11..98

Chapter 12..106

Chapter 13..117

Chapter 14.. 126

Chapter 15.. 135

Chapter 16..150

Chapter 17... 154

Chapter 18... 161

Chapter 19...166

Chapter 20... 176

Chapter 21...183

Feedback Request..197

Chapter 1

Sally wakes up to the ever-present sound of a symphony of baby coos, whining, and blankets being thrown from the crib. Jackson is nearly one year old and spirited. She opens her eyes to the light peeking in through the top of the curtains. Her husband, William, is already gone. A dent, the only evidence he slept next to her. Probably already working, she thinks.

She rolls out of bed so that all of her escapes simultaneously, feet finding the ground at the last moment. Even her feet wish for more sleep. She plods into the bathroom and begins to brush her teeth while she thinks of the day's to-dos.

As she thinks of her list, she wonders if William will have gotten the baby out of bed, but she knows. She knows he thinks of childcare as her responsibility, not his. The thought makes her grind her teeth, a feat with a toothbrush inside her mouth—an act of irritation.

She wanders to the nursery down the hall and around the corner and opens the door. Jackson is standing up in his crib, and almost everything is on the floor.

"Good morning, sweet boy," she says sweetly as she picks up all his blankies and stuffed animals in one sweeping motion. He squeals with delight as she picks him up. "Let's go get some breakfast."

Sally makes Jackson a bottle and herself a coffee; it is at this moment that she realizes she hasn't even seen her husband.

"William?" she calls. No answer. He must be working in the office down the hall and can't hear her. Maybe already gone, surely, he would have said goodbye. Wouldn't he? Oh, well. Jackson drinks his bottle as Sally sips her coffee while Elmo keeps them company on the television.

William wanders in, already dressed for the day, almost ready to walk out the door. "Good morning," he says.

"Morning!" She chirps and waves Jackson's chubby hand at his daddy. She notices his wrist rolls, *rubber band wrists,* she calls them, and makes a mental note to remember this. Her personal mental photo album.

"What do you all have planned for today?" he asks.

"Oh, you know, lots of exciting stuff. Saving the world," she quips. "Nothing really, actually. I might take him for a stroll later. If I can get some work done during his nap."

"Cool. Well, I've got to head out. Got to call on some doctors between surgeries." William works in medical sales and is rarely in the office. He goes from one doctor's office to another and often to hospitals during surgeries. He works mainly with orthopedists. He seems uninterested in Sally and Jackson's plans for the day, an unsurprising fact.

"I guess it's just us again, little buddy." William gives Sally and Jackson an equal kiss on the top of the head before he walks out the door.

Following breakfast Sally and Jackson play with blocks, do puzzles, and play with farm animals before his morning nap. During his morning nap, Sally does her very part-time work as a CPA for a small boutique down the street. She opens the spreadsheet the owner keeps in the cloud and scrolls through it for twenty minutes, looking for anything that might be out of place or incorrect. Numbers swirl in her head like a tornado, but to her, they all line up.

Numbers are linear, they make sense to Sally. Looks good, she thinks. She scrolls social media and sees several of her mother's friends have shared a post saying, "Share this post so your account won't be deleted." She rolls her eyes, groans, and exits social media all at once.

She wanders into her walk-in closet and finds her uniform: athleisure. More specifically, yoga pants and a workout top, sometimes topped with a pullover. She knows she is a stereotype, but they really are comfy, and she needs the ease of use of all her limbs when dealing with a toddler.

After Jackson's nap, Sally gets him dressed and wrestles him into his car seat, which makes her break a sweat. She then hits her head on the car door, trying to escape his clutches. Sweat now steadily prickles at her brow, and she knows there's more where that came from because she hasn't even packed up the stroller yet. Ordinarily, she takes Jackson on stroller rides in their neighborhood, but he's begun to get antsy in his stroller, so she decided to try a new walking trail to hold his attention. As they drive, Jackson babbles in the back seat. "I hear you, babe!" she wants him to know.

They arrive at Lakeview Park, and Sally gets the stroller, Jackson, her bag, his snack, and his sippy cup out of the car. By this time, she's definitely sweating. She removes her pullover before they have even begun to exercise. She gets him settled, puts in her air pods, fires up her playlist, and begins to walk. She can just barely hear Jackson jabbering through the music pumping through her ears, but she steadily marches on. The weather is surprisingly low in humidity, and she is glad she made an effort to come to this hiking trail. It was a task to get it all done, but she knows being outdoors will reap benefits for her and Jackson both. But mostly her.

She will be less likely to lose her patience with him. She thinks about his little face when she loses her patience, and the familiar feeling of mom guilt begins to wash over her. Guilt and shame, really. He has done nothing to deserve her irritated tone when it escapes her lips.

Out of the corner of her eye, she sees something beneath the brush several yards away. It is a stark contrast to the organic, earthy colors of the ground; an iconic, not-found-in-nature bubblegum pink. She hastens her pace, and the stroller goes bump-a-bump as they leave the trail and begin their jaunt on the uneven earth beneath them. She arrives at the color in question and gently jolts the pine needles, leaves, and mulch off what she sees with her white tennis shoe, and it comes into view clearly: a pink crescent-shaped purse.

"Cute," she said to herself, and Jackson by default.

"Ba ba ba ba," Jackson replies. He's ready for a bottle- she makes a mental note to hurry.

Sally meanders back to the trail and continues her walk. The pink bag stays in her mind. She is unable to shake it. But why? She tries to push it out of her mind, but it keeps returning. A flash of the pink bag as if it's deja vu. Then it dawns on her, and she inhales. Suddenly she remembers seeing a picture of a similar bag when she was scrolling Facebook this morning. The pink bag was on the description of a missing woman when she was last seen. Sally accelerates her pace to get to the end of the trail so she can turn around and make her way back to the purse in double time.

By the time she makes her way to the purse, she is nearly running. Jackson is starting to whine more pressingly, and she knows her invisible timer has begun. She spots the purse and lets out a sigh.

"Thank goodness it's still here," she says out loud. She reaches down and grabs a bag for dirty diapers- similar to a dog waste bag- and uses it as a makeshift glove. She wants to avoid getting her fingerprints on a piece of evidence, assuming it does belong to the missing woman. She only knows what she's seen on episodes of Dateline, 20/20, and plenty of Netflix documentaries. Still, she knows enough not to implicate herself in an obvious manner. She gently places the bag underneath the stroller and makes haste to get back to her car. Now she has more pressing matters than just the bottle for Jackson.

By the time she gets to the car, Jackson is moments away from wailing. At his current stage, he is whining incessantly. She plops Jackson in his car seat, mixes formula with water from her water bottle, and gives it to Jackson. He instantly quiets and guzzles the bottle. Now, to deal with this purse. She searches the car and finds an old Target bag used for car trash collection, hoping the purse will fit inside. She puts the same makeshift plastic baggy glove on her hand and, ever so gently, places the purse inside the Target bag. It fits. She ties the bag into a little bow, and then that feels silly, so she ties it into a tasteful, professional knot.

Chapter 2

Sally wants to drop Jackson right into his crib for his afternoon nap so she can throw herself into *research*, but she knows he deserves better. She gives him a pouch and some fruit for lunch, which he promptly throws on the ground. She reads him "The Very Hungry Caterpillar" while he swigs his bottle prior to his nap. She rocks him and sings, "You are my sunshine," while he lays his head on her shoulder. His breathing slows and he takes deep heavy sighs.

That was quick, she thinks. Children must innately know when their mothers have important work to do. But she's always heard the opposite. Either way, thank you precious Jackson. She gently lowers him into bed and holds her breath silently, wishing he won't wake. He doesn't (this time) and she sneaks out of his room.

Finally. She essentially runs to her computer and pulls up Facebook. This is a job that calls for a screen larger than her phone. She has to google how to find posts she's liked because she always forgets. She quickly scrolls through her likes and doesn't see it. "Damnit," she says audibly. The rest of the house is silent, and her words echo in the halls. Her own words startle her and make her feel like someone else is in the house with her.

Next, she searches for her local news station and immediately the picture of a woman pops up. "There she is," she says. The woman is young—early twenties, and every thirty- and forty-something-year-old man's dream. It's just a headshot, and it looks professional. She scrolls through the words of the post about the missing woman.

"Missing... Gina Thorpe... twenty-five... blonde hair... real estate agent... last seen two weeks ago..." She scrolls through the pictures on the post. Another picture of Gina, a picture of her car, and then she sees it. Stock photos of what she was last seen wearing. Along with the purse. The purse Sally has in her car.

Sally begins to shiver internally; her nervous system is processing what is happening before her conscious mind. Okay, you have a missing woman's purse, she tells herself. Okay this is not good. She tries to calm herself by taking a deep breath. It doesn't work. She curses herself for even walking over to the pink mound and then picking it up.

What were you thinking, Sally?! You weren't. *Curiosity killed the cat* is a saying for a reason. You dumb woman.

Right. Damaging self-talk isn't going to help. Let's get more information. Like with Sally's job, you need all the numbers to piece together a puzzle. Several numbers don't tell the whole story.

Similarly, just finding a missing woman's purse doesn't tell the whole story. She begins reading more about Gina. Can I call you Gina? Are we on a first-name basis now? She tries to make herself laugh. They might as well be friends, or at least make-believe friends, since Sally is now on Team Gina.

Sally learns that Gina is a real estate agent that works primarily with first-time homebuyers in a town over, Bainhill. She sounds professional and she's cute. She reads about the last place Gina was publicly seen: The Corner Vine, a restaurant just a few minutes away from her home. Sally gets a funny feeling in the pit of her stomach. The Corner Vine. William loves to eat lunch there. Just a coincidence, she assures herself.

Sally wonders if she should take the purse to the police. Of course, you should. She knows. Of course, she knows, but she also wonders. She pulls up the bank statements on her computer and then clicks over to William's debit card. She looks at them almost daily, to keep tabs on checks and balances.

She loves it when the money in/money out balances according to her calculations. When she was younger, she loved balancing a checkbook, but this is how she does it now. She scrolls through and sees nothing of consequence at first.

Then she sees it,

The Corner Vine- $56.80

The Corner Vine- $35.25

The Corner Vine- $67.23

Her stomach falls as if she's ridden a rollercoaster. Sally hates rollercoasters. She calms herself. It isn't illegal to go to lunch. Again, it could be a coincidence. She searches the date that Gina was last seen. Ah, there it is, March 27th. She really misses having her own office and two computer screens, or at least a cubicle. She goes back to the bank statements to cross-list the date. There it is. The Corner Vine on March 27th.

The answer to the calculation that she didn't want to see. Sally feels like she is going to vomit. The same feeling she had almost her entire pregnancy with Jackson. She stops, straightens her back, and rolls her shoulders back. This could all be an entire coincidence. There are plenty of people who live parallel lives to Sally and William.

This is nothing of consequence. She wonders how many people walk in and out of the doors of The Corner Vine daily. Hundreds, if not a thousand, on a busy day. William could have had lunch, and Gina could have had dinner. Simple as that. Easy peasy.

As if on cue, the baby monitor comes to life. Jackson begins to moan and roll around in his crib. Sally shuts her laptop and hears it slam with a thud. Harder than she meant to. She turns and looks over her shoulder, half expecting to see someone standing there, watching her. She glances back at the baby monitor and wonders if Jackson is now awake or if he will go back to sleep.

It's the daily gamble and she often bets with herself. If he goes back to sleep, you win ten bucks. She doesn't, but it's a game she plays with herself. She realizes in this moment she needs more mom friends. Jackson grabs his teddy bear and snuggles it. She thinks he will go back to sleep and then he sits straight up.

She thinks about the purse again and pushes the feelings of concern about William down, down, down. She might be able to trick her brain into thinking about other things, but her stomach has a mind of its own and the familiar ache is ever-present. She knows what she must do even though she doesn't want to. At all.

She doesn't want the police to suspect her husband. He might not be the perfect husband, but he is a good man. He is a kind man, an honest man, and Sally knows he would never hurt another living soul, least of all a woman.

She wonders if she should consult with William before going to the police. But she worries he will be upset with her if she does. Of course, he would be upset, anyone would be if they were accused of infidelity and involvement with a missing person. A missing person, the words vibrate in her brain.

As Sally enters Jackson's room, he immediately says, "Hi."

"Hi, sweet boy!" she says back to him.

"Nack, nack," he says. She is surprised he's already starting to talk, but she knows what this means. He's ready for a snack.

"Alright, buddy, let's go get a snack." He claps in response.

In the kitchen Sally places Jackson in his highchair and gives him an applesauce pouch, his favorite. Sally wishes she didn't have to do this, but she knows she must. She still wonders if this is the right thing to do, if she is betraying her husband. She pulls out her phone and texts the babysitter.

She quickly replies she can be over in thirty minutes. She was half hoping the babysitter would be busy and unavailable. Thirty minutes for Sally's anxiety to swell and pull her heart underwater.

Chapter 3

Sally takes a deep breath and starts her car. She begins to drive not knowing what she will say once she gets to the police station. Um, I found this purse and I believe it belongs to a dead person? Obviously can't say that. I think I found a missing woman's bag? That sounds more like it. She wonders if there is a specific police station that keeps evidence or if it's a station-to-station kind of thing. Do they all have evidence lockers? Are they franchised? Is it like Chick-Fil-A?

She pulls up to the police station and it's all brick with some low-cost (she assumes) white tile and mostly ugly. All the federal buildings in Ashbrook were built in the seventies and it shows. They could certainly use a little sprucing, but she doesn't want to finance that. She realizes she is trying to keep her mind off what she is there to do. Her brain is protecting her.

She finds a parking spot that isn't labeled, which is more difficult than you would think, and parks. She gets out of her car and almost walks through the doors without the bag. The bag within a bag. Gina's bag inside the Target bag. She whips around and pulls in out of her backseat. She walks through the metal detector and gives a polite and nondescript smile to the attendant. He seems uninterested in her existence.

Sally walks up to the first manned desk she can find. There is a woman sitting at it. She has dark skin and a short, cropped haircut. She looks like she means business and Sally is instantly intimidated. "Um, hello. I'd like to drop off something I found that I think might be important."

"And what exactly do you have that you think might be important?" The woman asks in an almost accusatory tone. Her name tag says *Sanders*. Sally didn't know how Sanders had to fight and claw through each day as a woman in law enforcement. It toughened her.

"I think I found a bag that belongs to a missing woman, Gina Thorpe. I'm not actually sure it's hers, but it looks like the one I saw on the news." She stumbles through her words.

"Hold on one second," Officer (Agent?) Sanders says. Her entire demeanor changes. She picks up the phone. "Hey, tell King to come to the front desk ASAP." She hangs up the phone with a thunk.

A few moments later a short, stocky man walks around the corner and almost imperceptibly looks at Sanders and then Sanders looks at Sally. Sally notices and then looks to the ground, but before she can look to the ground, her eyes catch the Target bag in her hands. Again, her stomach drops.

"Detective King. Come with me." He says, sticking out his hand to shake Sally's.

"Hi, I'm Sally Parker." Detective Bobby King nods and starts walking. Sally follows him into a small room. She assumes this must be an interrogation room. Her nerves are vibrating even more so than before she walked in, a feeling she didn't know was possible.

"So, Sally. What can I do for you?" Detective King asks.

"I found a purse. And I think it might belong to Gina Thorpe, the missing woman." She pats the Target bag that is now sitting on the table between them.

"I'm the detective on the case. Have you touched the purse that you found?" He asks.

"I haven't. I put a little baggie on my hand and then put it right in this bag. I thought I recognized it, but I know it might not be hers. I wanted to bring it in just in case." She feels sheepish explaining this to him, a professional at solving crime.

"So, tell me where you found it."

Sally took a deep breath. This is it, she thought. Be aware of what you say and how you say it. Now you're taking too long to get started. Just get on with it! "I took my son on a stroller ride at Lakeview Park. About halfway through our walk, I noticed something pink under the brush. I went over and saw it and picked it up. I remembered seeing it on the news and I thought I would bring it here to you."

"That's it?" he asked.

"That's it." She said.

"Okay thanks for that information. How old is your son?" Detective King asked. He thought he could get her talking by asking about the son she mentioned.

"He's almost one. Well, he's eleven months, actually." She said smiling, thinking of her sweet boy. She tapped her phone on the table to show Detective King her background, which is a picture of Jackson.

"Cute kid. Why'd you pick to go to Lakeview Park?" He asked quick, rapid-fire questions. It gave her barely enough time to think about what her answer would be. He wasn't new at this. He had been a detective for nearly twenty years.

"We usually walk around our neighborhood. We live in Westport. But my son, Jackson, has been restless on our stroller rides lately, so I wanted to try somewhere new. We had never been there before."

"Nice neighborhood. You married?" He asked.

"I am. My husband, William, is in medical sales." Her stomach dropped when he asked about William. Did he, too, suspect William?

"How long have you been married?"

"Almost five years. We waited a few years before having children."

"I think you know that you messed up by picking it up, don't you?" He said.

"I realize now that wasn't my best idea. I'm sorry. I hope this doesn't throw a wrench in your investigation." She feels embarrassed.

"Not much of an investigation right now. Nothing to go off. Until now. Until you." He said ominously.

"Oh really? Did I crack the case?" Sally smirked, feeling sure of herself.

"Not exactly. But at least now we have some evidence. I can't tell you anything else right now. But thanks for bringing this in. We're going to need to fingerprint you just in case your prints did get on the purse during transfer. You good with that?"

"Oh, I wasn't expecting that. But yes, of course. I will do anything I can to help."

"Great. Sanders will get that started for you."

Sally felt like a criminal getting fingerprinted. Sanders is rough with her hands, but Sally senses a kindness in her. She wants to talk to her and ask her about her life, her family, but she knows it's inappropriate. Maybe in another life, another situation, they could be friends. Not likely.

But this is a vice of her own making. She knows she shouldn't have picked up that purse, so why did she? A question for her therapist. On her drive home, she thinks about the day behind her. It was certainly unexpected, yet a bit exciting. A smile creeps across her face.

Then she shakes it off. It isn't right to find delight in the misfortune of others, she thinks. Her mother used to say that to her when she was a child. She thinks about what could have happened to Gina: a mugging gone wrong, kidnapped by someone she was showing a house to, or even running away and creating a new identity. But why? That question lingers in her mind.

She gets home and the babysitter says everything was good, other than Jackson's diaper rash. Back to reality, she thinks. Again, she wonders why she's so excited by figuring out what happened to Gina. She isn't a crime fighter, not really. It seems like everyone listens to true crime podcasts and watches the documentaries these days. Everyone is just bored and entertained by gruesome facts, the worse the better. She feels ashamed that she's interested, especially given the uncomfortable fact that Gina and William almost definitely crossed paths.

Sally looks at the clock and realizes there isn't much time left until dinner. She looks at her list of dinners she has planned for the week on her phone and decides on the very boring chicken and rice for supper. William loves it and it will be easy to share with Jackson.

She begins chopping onions and Jackson fusses at her feet. This won't be easy, she thinks. She scoops him up and goes to the garage to get her baby carrier. She straps it on her midsection and buckles him in. He is happiest being worn by her, but she worries he will get burned by hot oil. Risk and reward, she thinks.

Halfway through making dinner, William walks through the door. "Daddy's home!" Sally says while unbuckling Jackson and handing him directly to William. She gives him a little kiss to welcome him and make his welcome home present, holding a fussy baby, sweeter. He doesn't say anything, but she can tell by his air that he is irritated.

He wants to get in the door and have a seat before stepping in for his parental duties. But sometimes it doesn't work like that. He has no idea what's to come, but she will wait to discuss the day's events with him when the baby is asleep. It won't be long now.

William and Jackson gobble up their dinner in record time while Sally nibbles and sips her Syrah.

Jackson does the sign for *more* from his highchair, so Sally hops up and gives him more chicken and white rice, his favorite. She smiles as she sits, and Jackson smirks, as he throws his food on the ground. "Oh, Jackson," she says. "Are you all done? When you throw your food, that means all done!"

Jackson does that sign for *all done*. She stands back up, her muscles tensing. She knows they are yearning for a break from the constant up and down.

"Do you want me to get his bath started or you?" she asks William.

"You," he says. "I'll clean up dinner."

Sally is relieved because watching Jackson splash in the tub is more fun than scrubbing dishes. Bath time comes and goes, and Sally begins the bedtime routine. She coats Jackson in lotion, puts his pickup truck pajamas on, and takes him to his room. She reads him several books, gives him a bottle, rocks and sings to him, and puts him in bed. "Night, night," she says. He waves to her with his pudgy hand. He's so tired he doesn't even fight it. He grabs his teddy and snuggles in soft and deep.

Sally feels butterflies in her stomach as she knows what she's about to tell William. When she gets downstairs, she finds him drinking a beer and watching sports in the living room. "So. Something a little bit interesting happened today." She tells him.

"Oh yeah?" He says but sounds half uninterested.

"Yeah. We went on a stroller ride at Lakeview Park, and I found a purse. A purse that belongs to a missing woman." She says.

"A what?!" William's volume rises with the conversation. He's interested now. He's looking at her with inquisition in his eyes.

"I know. Have you heard of the missing woman, Gina Thorpe?" she asks nonchalantly to check his temperature on the subject. He looks down at his beer.

"No, I haven't. Who is she?"

"She's younger than us. But she's missing. So anyway, I think the purse I found belongs to her. I took it to the police station," She says.

"You went to the police station today? I did not expect any of this." He seems bothered that she didn't tell him, or at least that is her assumption. But he, too, didn't check in with her all day.

"I didn't either, William! I have been totally freaking out! I didn't touch the purse, but they did fingerprint me, so that was kind of weird. Look at my hands!" She shows him the now gray residue on her fingertips.

"Oh, Sally, no. No. No, you didn't let them do that." He says.

"What? I didn't do anything, so it's fine." She shrugs and meets his eyes.

"Good God, Sally. Now they're going to try to say you did it." William says while he runs his hands over his face. His tell for when he is stressed beyond what his brain can handle, and his body takes over.

"But I didn't do it, William. I literally just found her purse and I wanted to help. Why are you being such a dick?" She feels her face turning red. She is defensive because she wonders if there is something William isn't telling her. A wife always knows.

"I'm not being a dick; I'm trying to protect you."

"From what?" She asks, and he walks out of the room. His silence speaks volumes.

Chapter 4

Two days later, everything is back to normal. Sally and William are pretending like nothing happened, but concern prickles at her palms from time to time. Could William be involved? He certainly didn't say, "I didn't do it," but she also didn't ask. She should ask him. But she is scared she will get an answer that she doesn't want or doesn't know how to handle.

How did finding a purse turn into such a tricky situation? Again, she wishes she had walked past the purse. She yearns for a time when her days were more boring. Where are you Gina, she says to herself often. As her mind wanders to Gina, her phone rings.

Sally doesn't know the number, but she answers. "Hello?" She wonders why she always answers like a question.
"Sally, hi. This is Detective Bobby King."
"Oh hi, Detective King. How are you?" She says. Her stomach drops when she recognizes his voice.

"Fine. I have a few more questions to ask you about what you saw. Could you come in today so we can talk?" He asks.

"Hold on, let me look at my calendar." She pulls up her calendar on her phone and sees that she has a playdate planned for this afternoon after nap time, but tomorrow there is free. She knows skirting around the police is a surefire way to be implicated, so she will go. She wonders if she should tell William or not. She doesn't want to start another fight. "Alright, I'm actually busy today, but I can come tomorrow. How about 9:30?"

"Works for me. See you then." He hangs up without saying goodbye. Some might find his behavior rude, but Sally has worked with businessmen enough to know that this is just how they operate: short and succinct.

Following the phone call, Sally gets herself and Jackson ready for the playdate. It's a new friend, a woman she really doesn't know. Her name is Nicole and her husband, Michael, works with William. It feels like a setup but that's fine because Sally definitely does need more friends.

She has her best friend, Katherine, and a few other friends here and there, but no other friends with kids. They texted sporadically over the course of a month and finally agreed on a day and time to meet with the children at a park not too far from home.

They arrive at the park and Sally feels like she is on a first date. What if she doesn't like me, she thinks. And then is embarrassed that she cares. She looks around and realizes she has absolutely no clue what Nicole looks like. She could have purple hair and Sally wouldn't have the foggiest idea.

Sally sees a woman walking up to her from quite a distance away, and she feels butterflies in her stomach. The woman is tall and lean, with long brown straight hair, the kind you don't have to blow dry. She's younger than Sally imagined, much younger, she would venture to guess.

"Hi, are you Sally? I'm Amanda, Nicole's nanny."

"Yes, I am. Hi Amanda, nice to meet you." Sally said with surprise and reached out a hand to meet Amanda. She didn't say what she wanted to; Hi Amanda, your boss is rude as hell. She didn't even text Sally to let her know she would be sending a stand-in.

"I'm not sure if Nicole let you know, but she had some things pop up, so she just sent me along instead," Amanda explained, pointing to the two children already playing with Jackson. They looked to be around one and a half and three years old. Sally noticed a bird tattoo on Amanda's wrist and she wondered what it meant.

"She didn't, but I'm glad to meet you," Sally said.
"You looked totally surprised," said Amanda.

"To be honest with you, I was. Nothing against your boss, but I was expecting to see her. Michael and my husband, William, work together."
"I've never even met Michael!" Amanda blurted out and then half-heartedly tried to cover her mouth. Sally and Amanda both awkwardly l

"Twenty-two," so young, but Sally feels a connection to her. All while they're talking, the children will come to them for a snack or a sip of water and then go back to playing. The interruptions don't stop their conversation. An hour into their playdate, Amanda and Sally are laughing and chatting like they've known each other for years. Amanda is pleasantly surprised that Sally accepts her, and Sally is energized by Amanda's youthfulness and willingness to connect with her. Amanda tells Sally about her boyfriend back in Washington and how he still texts her, begging for her to come back. By the end of the play date, they exchange numbers and plan to meet again next week.

That night Sally's routine is commonplace. When she and William are lying in bed, she rolls over towards him. "I don't want to get in a fight, William. But I do feel like I need to ask you: did you have anything to do with Gina Thorpe going missing? I know you didn't, but I still feel like I need to ask." She says it all in one breath.

"How can you even ask me that, Sally?" He doesn't get angry but instead sounds sad.

"I know you didn't. But what you said the other day, I felt like I needed to ask."

"I get it," he says. He scoots over and begins kissing her, putting his hands on the familiar parts he likes most.

Chapter 5

Sally feels anxious the entire time leading up to going to the police station. She wonders if she should tell Amanda about what she found and how it has led to her spending time at the police station.

She wonders if Amanda has ever been to jail- it isn't out of the question. Detective King is intimidating, and she's afraid he will ask her a question she doesn't have the answer to. It's acceptable to say, "I don't know," she reminds herself.

Sally pulls up to the police station and zooms into the same parking spot as before. She is a creature of habit. She walks up to Sanders's desk and says hello. Sanders says nothing but instead stands up and walks toward the same room Sally and Detective King had sat in the previous time. Sally wonders, do I follow her? She quickly decides to follow Sanders. "Why are you following me?" Sanders asks.

"Oh, sorry. I thought you wanted me to follow you to that room." She is beyond embarrassed.

"No. I'm going to get King." Sanders wants to roll her eyes, so much so that they begin to roll all on their own. She must blink to make them stop.

"Oh okay. I'm so sorry." She feels her chest turning red and can feel it rising like the tide. She sheepishly goes back to the makeshift lobby and finds a seat. She pulls out her phone and realizes she has nothing to look at. She doesn't even feel like playing Candy Crush - is this what depression feels like? She locks it and puts it back in her bag.

"Sally." Detective King comes around the corner.

"Hi." She says back. No pleasantries after that embarrassing lapse in judgment. Keep your words to a minimum, she tells herself. Sally follows Detective King to the same room. This time she knows she is supposed to. They walk in and sit down, one on each side of the table. The room feels colder and more sterile this time.

Detective King's demeanor matches the room. Sally can tell he has something specific to ask her.

"So, Sally, I had a few questions about where you found the purse and whatnot," he says.

"I understand."

"Now. When you found the purse, did you see anything out of the ordinary? Any cars around? Any suspicious activity? We're trying to piece this thing together."

"Yeah, sure, let me think about this... I don't think I saw anything unusual. I had my air pods in, so I couldn't really hear anything other than my son kind of whining. It was a little bit weird that the purse wasn't too far off the trail, and it wasn't covered well at all."

"Thanks. So, nothing unusual there. What about before you started walking? Did you see anyone, talk to anyone, or see any vehicles?"

"I didn't talk to anyone. I make it a point to be aware of my surroundings when I'm alone with the baby. I didn't see anything out of the ordinary. I'm trying to remember if I even saw any other walkers, but I can't remember if I did or not. I probably would have remembered that because it makes me a little bit nervous, like I said, when I'm on my own with the baby."

"Got it. So, Sally, let me ask you this: why did you go over to the purse and leave and then come back to it?" He raised one eyebrow as he asked it.

Sally was stunned. How did they know she had gone to the purse and returned to it? She wonders if her mouth has fallen open because she certainly feels dumbfounded. She clenches her jaw as a reminder that her chin is right where it belongs.

"We checked the security cameras at the park," he answered her question without her ever uttering it out loud.

"I...um, I... I," Sally found herself stuttering, which was incredibly uncommon for her. She was astounded.

"Do you have anything else you want to tell me, Sally?" he asked.

"Oh my goodness, Detective King. I think you have the wrong idea. I saw the purse and then after seeing it for the first time remembered where I had seen it before. Nothing more, nothing less. Then I went back to grab it to bring it to you guys. Surely you saw on the camera that I picked it up exactly the way I told you I did?" She hoped she sounded genuine.

"We did see that. We also saw that you didn't initially put it inside the Target bag, so that means the integrity of our evidence is shot to hell." He no longer sounds kind, friendly, or the least bit cordial. Did Sally see him roll his eyes? "I'm going to step out for a moment, and I'll be back. Do you want a cup of coffee?"

"That sounds great, thanks," Sally said, unclear on how she was able to maintain composure at this moment. It seems like he suspects Sally, but maybe he is solely upset because she did not handle the evidence to his standards. She takes a deep breath and reminds herself she didn't do anything wrong.

She also remembers that there are cameras in these types of rooms so as not to move her hands in any way that might make her look guilty. For heaven's sake, she was just trying to help him. She begins to wonder if he's an incompetent ass.

Detective Bobby King returns with two steaming plastic cups full of coffee and sets them on the table. He inches Sally's towards her. She takes a small sip, realizes this is terrible coffee, and puts it down.

"I want to apologize for not handling the evidence correctly, Detective King. I know I didn't do the right thing at that moment, and I would go back and change it if I could. But I can't, and I want to help you in any way I can."

"Sally, did you know that the last place Gina Thorpe was seen was The Corner Vine? The same place your husband eats lunch multiple times a week?"

Sally debates whether she should be truthful. She chooses to play dumb. "I didn't know that, Detective."

She tries to act surprised. She feels like a bad actress, but she thinks he falls for it.

"Well, she did. That's where Gina ate her last known meal. A restaurant your husband is known to frequent. So, I've asked myself: is it a coincidence that Sally Parker found Gina Thorpe's missing purse, or did she plant it there? And you know what I think, Sally? I think you're smarter than people think you are, even your own husband. You're a smart lady and I think you figured out what was going on between Gina and William. Just like I figured it out. It wasn't hard to find the parallels between them. And I think you took matters into your own hands. And now you've found yourself in a predicament you don't know how to get out of, not for lack of trying."

Sally gasps, and her hand covers her mouth as he says the words.

Chapter 6

It has become immediately apparent to Sally that Detective King believed she had something to do with the missing woman, Gina Thorpe. Not just something to do with it, but the perpetrator.

How could he think that Sally is a criminal? Ridiculous, at least to her. He doesn't even know her, and she wonders the extent of his education. She doesn't doubt his competence, she would never insult a professional, but she wonders about his percentage of solving cases versus cold cases and if this statistic is public record.

Sally walks out of the police station, wondering what the next hours, days and weeks of her life will look like. She has heard that once the police suspect you, they will make the evidence fit their theory. This thought terrifies and immobilizes her. She thinks of leaving her husband and son, wearing a jumpsuit, and eating from a tray in a cold metal industrial cafeteria. Tears prickle in the corners of her eyes, and she feels her chin quiver.

She no longer has control of her emotions, and this is the moment where she gives in to them or takes control. This time, she gives in and lets the tears fall. She is afraid.

She falls into her car like a pile of laundry being dropped. She doesn't care who sees her or what cameras watch her. At this moment, she feels defeated and exhausted. She wants to talk to someone. Needs to talk to someone. She isn't in the mood to be scolded for her role in her personal situation, so she knows William is not who to call. She thinks of her best friend, her dearest friend, Katherine, and pulls up her number from her favorites.

Ba-ring, ba-ring.

"Helloooo!" Katherine says in her usual upbeat and chirpy tone.

"Hey," Sally replies. She sounds even more depressed than she feels.

"What's wrong?" Katherine's tone immediately falls to meet Sally's.

"I'm in such a mess," Sally says, immediately bursting into tears again. The words begin spilling out of her. "Last week, I found this purse at the park. Well, it turns out it belongs to a missing woman and now the cops think I have something to do with it. But I don't. I swear I don't. Please believe me, Kat, I didn't have anything to do with this." She confesses without taking a breath.

"Whoa, whoa, whoa. Slow down. Let's meet up for coffee. Can you do that? Where's the baby?"

"Yes, let's do that. Beans and Things on Beckingham. I have a sitter."

Sally tries to calm herself as she drives silently to the coffee shop. She even turns the radio off which is highly unusual for her. She listens to the engine whirr and the wheels meet the pavement as her mind spins and her breath returns to normal. She thinks about Katherine and her husband, Jason. Katherine is in marketing, and Jason is a divorce attorney.

The irony is that they almost divorced after only being married for a year, but they worked it out. They had not yet had children. The conversation between Katherine and Sally had come up organically, as all their conversations do. Katherine was flip-flopping between having children and not, and Jason was neutral on the subject, which struck Sally as odd.

Sally's mind is elsewhere, so much so that she almost misses the entry to the coffee shop, even with the massive sign right beside her. She shakes her head like a wet dog shaking off water and pulls into the parking lot.

Inside Beans and Things Sally scans the room for Katherine. She spots her at the far corner bistro table with a large coffee cup in front of her and one in the spot that Sally will soon occupy. Sally walks over to the table and greets Katherine.

"Hi," Sally says. Katherine hops up and gives Sally a little squeeze around the shoulders. Katherine's version of a hug.

"Hey. Tell me what's going on. Start from the beginning." Katherine places her chin in her hands, always ready for a story.

Sally takes an audibly deep breath as she begins to tell her tale. "It all started last week when I took Jackson on a stroller ride at the park. A stroller ride! My demise is coming from a stroller ride. Oh, God." She gets back on track. "Anyway, I saw something and went to grab it. It was a pink purse. I knew it looked familiar, so I grabbed it with a baggy and put it inside a Target bag. Well, imagine my surprise when I realized this purse belonged to a missing woman. I knew it looked familiar, but I couldn't remember why. When I got home, I got on Facebook and found the picture right there."

"Wow. Who is the woman?" Sally was astounded that that was Katherine's only question.

"Her name is Gina Thorpe. Have you heard of her?"

"I heard a woman was missing, but I don't know anything else." Katherine's brow furrowed as she processed the words she was listening to, and Sally could see the wheels turning in her head.

"Well, I'll tell you what I've found out about her. She is a real estate agent. And here's the weird thing... I feel so bad saying this but... the last place she was seen was The Corner Vine. And Katherine, do you know who eats lunch there almost every day of the workweek?"

Katherine's eyes nearly doubled in size. Her reaction was the answer to Sally's question. She continued. "I know. I can't help but be suspicious. I know in my heart he didn't do anything, but it feels like a little bit too much of a coincidence."

"That is interesting. I think we both know William didn't have anything to do with it. I mean, how would he even have time? He's always working, isn't he?"

Katherine and Sally both knew Kat's comment was half-joke, half-truth. Sally nodded knowingly.

"Anyway," Sally continued, "I took the purse to the police station, and now all of a sudden, the idiot detective thinks I have something to do with it."

"Why in the world would he think that?"

"He seems to think that... that...." Sally's chin began to quiver, and her voice cracked. "He thinks that William and Gina were having an affair." A sob choked her, and she covered her face with her hands. Her shoulders moved up and down.

"Oh, sweetie," Katherine consoled her and patted her hand. "We'll get through this. We'll figure this out together. I promise! I'm not going to let anything happen to you."

Sally's sobs slowed down and she sniffed. She didn't have a tissue, so she wiped her nose on her sleeve like a child. She nods her head in a delayed reaction to what Katherine has said. "I know, and I don't truly think they were having an affair. But I'm not sure. Not sure enough to believe him. I mean, things have changed since Jackson was born. I feel bad saying that, but it's true."

"Do you want me to talk to Jason about it or leave it between us?" Asked Katherine.

"Between us for now."

"Of course, whatever you want. He isn't here anyway. He's out of town for a trial."

The two women sip their coffee, no more words necessary to fill the space between them. Their friendship does not have awkward silences. Nothing needs to fill the space between them. Sally has no energy for more words, and Katherine is processing what she's just heard. They finish their coffee and walk out of the shop together, stepping into stride collectively.

"Keep me posted. On everything," Katherine says.

"I will," Sally nods.

Chapter 7

Sally's phone rings as she works on managing the numbers for Pink, the boutique she does accounting for. She notices the number but doesn't immediately place it. Then her stomach does a somersault as she realizes it's the police station: Detective King. Begrudgingly she picks up the phone, "Hello?" she asks with trepidation.

"Sally. Detective King." No pleasantries, Sally thinks.

"Hello, how are you?" Sally is being polite. She doesn't care how King is. In fact, she despises him.

"Fine. We just got Gina Thorpe's bank statements, and the last place she used her credit card was in Lake Littlejohn. But you probably already knew that didn't you?" He trails off. His persistent mind games aren't enough to crack Sally, and that's assuming there was something to crack; she reminds herself she has no part in this crime.

"Oh really? That's odd. I thought it was at The Corner Vi-"

"That's the last place she was seen. This is the last place her card was used." Detective King cuts her off. "Have you or your husband been there lately? It's a quaint little town."

"No, we haven't. In fact, I've never been there."

"I'm going to need some proof of that. Bank statements, cell phone data, something. It's called an alibi. Get one." He hangs up abruptly, leaving Sally with the phone to her ear. She pulls it away and stares at it in dismay as if the device insulted her. She knows now that she must bring William into the discussion and dreads it. Picking her phone back up, she silently wishes it won't work so she doesn't have to make this phone call. The screen comes to life immediately as if to taunt her.

William picks up on the first ring. "Hello?"

"Hi, babe. How's your day going?" Sally says.

"Oh, it's good, just working away. What's going on with you?"

"Well, I just got a call from Detective King. He said the last place Gina Thorpe was seen was in Lake Littlejohn. I told him we hadn't been there recently." Sally says.

"Okay." William says ominously.

"He said we need to give him proof."

"I can't believe we're still doing this. This is beyond ridiculous, but if it's proof that brute needs, I can give it to him. I can print out my timecards from checking in and out of the hospital with my badge. It keeps a record of how often I've been there so I can do my billing."

"Oh William, good! This is just what I needed to hear! I am so relieved. I can also print out our bank statements showing that we were here in town and not there on the dates in question. The dates are the week of March 27th. Just get them for the whole week, then we'll be in the clear."

"Got it. I'll take ti down to the police station myself."

"Sounds good. Oh, I'm so relieved. I hope this whole thing can be behind us after this."

"Me too."

"Oh, and William?"

"Yes?"

"Thank you."

Sally hangs up and pulls out her phone to text Katherine.

That dumb detective called again. He won't let it go that we have something to do with it. But we have proof that we were here. William has timecards, and I have bank statements for both of us. Hopefully, this will end this whole thing and I can go back to my boring life.

Katherine doesn't immediately text back, so she starts another text to her new friend, Amanda. They've had a few play dates with the children after their first meeting. Sally loves how eccentric Amanda is and doesn't sugarcoat anything. She also shamelessly loves that

Amanda gives her all the dirty details on Nicole's home life and how anti-perfect it is.

Hey- want to take the kids to the park this afternoon?

Amanda immediately responds. *Let's do it. Meet you there at 3.*

As she pushes the stroller to the park, Sally wonders what she should tell Amanda. She doesn't know her very well and doesn't want Amanda to judge her. But also wonders if Amanda has ever been to jail. She strikes Sally as the type of woman where nothing is beyond the realm of possibility. Turning into the playground gates, she sees Amanda smiling and waving at her.

"Hi, how are you?" Sally greets Amanda with a warm smile.

"Apparently better than you. You look tired." Amanda doesn't intend to pacify Sally, or anyone, with her words.

"Well, I guess I might as well tell you what's been going on." Amanda's eyes widen with the words that escape Sally's lips. She doesn't know if it's right to trust Amanda, but her gut tells her this is a safe space. Her gut also told her to pick up the purse, which has not gone well. She tries not to second guess herself, but with how her life has been turned upside down, she cannot help but pause.

"I found the purse of a missing woman, and now I'm under suspicion." Sally continues, "I had nothing to do with it! I am just the unluckiest person in the world, and now this detective thinks I planted it."

"Um... wow. I did not predict you to say that at all." Amanda says with a laugh.

"How could you be laughing right now?"

"Because it's hilarious! No offense, but you are the most vanilla person I've met since I've lived here. And here you are in the middle of a missing person investigation."

"Wow, that hurts. But I appreciate your honesty."

"Sorry, but it's facts, baby."

"Hopefully, we will get this figured out in the next week or so because the detective said he needs an alibi, which I have, yet he still seems to suspect me. Or William. Anyway, I have a question, and I hope I'm not crossing any boundaries for you. But I was wondering if you had ever been arrested?" Sally's volume lowered as she said the words. She was ashamed to be asking Amanda and didn't want to make assumptions based on a few tattoos. That would be an assumption her mother would make. "Tattoos don't make you a criminal, Mother," she'd tell her mother.

"I totally got arrested once! It was so dumb." Amanda was flippant in her response.

"Really? What was it like? I'm terrified this detective will try to pin this whole thing on me, and I didn't even know this woman." Sally was able to control herself this time when she spoke about it.

"It was so moronic. It was after a night out with friends, and you know some cops are just looking to pin somebody down. Well, I was stumbling to my car, and that's my bad. I shouldn't have done that. But I wasn't even going to drive! Or maybe I was. I don't actually remember. I'm pretty sure I wasn't going to drive, and I was just going to sit in my car and wait for my friend to pick me up. In any event, the cop walks up to me, shines his light directly in my eyes, and tells me to get out of the car. He tried to breathalyze me, and I said no. Did you know you can say no? Most people don't know that, but you can. You totally can. Then he wanted to search my car, and I said no to that too. That apparently made him really mad. So, he said he was arresting me for public intox- that's public intoxication- and I had to spend the night in jail. It ended up being basically nothing."

"Wow," Sally said. She didn't know what else to say. "So, was it scary being in jail?"

"It wasn't that big of a deal. I was only there for a few hours, and they put me in a tiny little cell by myself, so I wasn't actually scared for my safety or anything. I took a nap and then woke up and went home. But that cop was a dick."

"I hope it doesn't come to that. But I really think this detective has it out for me. He thinks William and the missing woman were having an affair."

"I'm pretty sure Nicole's husband is having an affair," Amanda said, changing the subject.

"WHAT?! Spill."

"He's never there! Sometimes when I get there in the mornings, he isn't there either. And I'm pretty sure he isn't working. The other day I came in, and it was really obvious that Nicole had been crying. I feel bad for her. It seems like he is not a good guy at all. He definitely isn't a good father. The kids never even mention him."

At their mere mention, the children begin to swarm the women like bees. Sally looks at her phone and realizes it is almost five p.m. which means dinnertime is quickly approaching, and it shows in the children. They whine and ask to be held. It is obvious to the women that their time together is coming to a close, so they say their goodbyes and buckle the children in their various clasps, whether in a car seat or stroller.

William walks into the home in a flurry of anger, speed, and testosterone. Jackson was already asleep and had been for hours. "Do you know what that detective said to me?" He seethes, his anger looking for anywhere to land and catapulting onto Sally. "He said that he knows that I was having an affair with Gina Thorpe, and he was going to prove it come hell or high water."

"Whoa, William. Well, what did you say?" Sally asks in a neutral tone.

"I almost punched him in the face but restrained myself for you and Jackson. Then I told him I don't have time for an affair with the amount I'm working. And then I told him if he wants to talk to either of us again, he will have to go through our lawyer."

Seeing William so passionate was exciting for Sally, but she held on to his words. Lawyer. She wondered if this was good. She didn't want to further anger Detective King, but she knew William was right. They needed to be protected. A lawyer could keep them safe in the legal sense.

"Thank you, William. I'm so sorry I got us into this mess." Her chin began to quiver. She always cried in the presence of her husband because she felt safe with him. Especially when she thought he was protecting her. She kissed him long and slow, and he grunted. Their night was just beginning.

Chapter 8

Sally's phone buzzed, and she peeled her body away from William's. It was a text message from Katherine: *Want to go on a walk today?* She responded immediately: *Yes, I'll text you after Jackson's morning nap and we can all go.*

She wanted to make sure Kat knew Jackson would be in attendance. Kat loved Jackson, but Sally wondered if she was always agreeable with him being around. He was so young they could talk about anything in front of him, and he had no clue. But it was more difficult with him around. Sally only had a few options for childcare other than a sporadic babysitter that she didn't even want to try today.

Her parents lived several hours away, and her in-laws were always busy with one fundraiser or another or an exotic trip. She loved them, but they definitely weren't baby people, and she understood that. She only asked for their help, specifically her mother-in law, Janice's help, when she was desperate.

Her father-in-law, Bruce, usually sat on the couch and watched the steady news stream on the television. He always seemed uninterested in the baby or anything else for that matter. He was a retired banker and was every bit the part. Her phone buzzed again with another text from Kat: *Perfect*.

Katherine drove to Sally's home after Jackson's nap, and they walked around Sally's neighborhood. Sally loved the mature trees, which offered shade on a sunny day, and the painted brick houses. She admired them all as they walked, and she wondered if Kat wished to live in a neighborhood like this. It seemed that she didn't.

She and Jason loved living in the bright lights of downtown in their townhouse just off Main Street. They lived a much more spontaneous and vibrant life, but Sally loved that they were different yet the same.

Sally remembered when they were children, and they would ride their bikes around the neighborhood they grew up in. One day they saw a dead cat in the middle of the road. Sally stopped and looked at it. She had to yell at Katherine to stop to even notice it. Katherine was flippant about the dead cat and told Sally that a car had probably hit it. Sally was traumatized by seeing it lying there, tongue hanging out of its mouth.

Katherine, seeing Sally upset, came to her rescue. She comforted her and told her it would be alright but that they had to go. This was a snapshot into their relationship, Kat coming to save Sally. Kat never needed saving. Sally wondered why this specific image and memory had come to her mind. She felt weak in their relationship, though since William had confronted Detective King, she felt stronger. There was a part of her waiting for the other shoe to drop, so to speak, in retaliation by the detective, but she tried to push those ideas out of her head.

"You won't believe what William did," Sally said. She didn't give Kat a chance to guess, ponder, or ask. "He went to the police station and got into a verbal altercation with Detective King. Or at least that's the story he told me."

"Go, William," Kat said, sounding surprised.

"I know. I was a little bit surprised too. He's usually so agreeable. Then he told me this part. He actually told Detective King not to speak to us again unless it was through our lawyer. I think he asked Jason who to use."

"Finally, you listen to legal advice. Good." Kat emphasized the good in an authoritative tone.

"So, I hope this is the end of this whole saga. I know this sounds terrible, but after this nightmare, I don't even want to know what happened to that poor woman. That's terrible, isn't it?"

"It isn't terrible. You didn't know her. You don't know her. And this thing has turned your world upside down. You don't owe her anything."

"Thanks. So, what's up with you? How are you? How is Jason?"

"Good. I'm bored. Jason is out of town again. He has this trial that has been lasting for weeks. I like to go with him when he has to work out of town for long stretches, but I can't because I've had so many meetings lately."

"Oh, really? Where is he this time?"

"Lake Littlejohn."

Sally wanted to stop walking. She wanted to let her jaw hit the floor. But she didn't. She walked on as if she didn't know what that meant. Lake Littlejohn. The same town where Gina Thorpe's credit card was last used. Sally knew this meant she wasn't finished thinking about Gina.

Following their walk, Sally thought tirelessly about Gina Thorpe. Where she might be, what she might have done, and what might have happened to her. She felt she didn't have anyone she could talk to about this. Kat would be furious if she knew that she suspected Jason. If she wasn't furious, she would be worried sick that he was having an affair, just as Sally had been when she thought the same thing about her own marriage.

William would scold her for digging and tell her to stay away from anything that has to do with Gina Thorpe completely. But Sally knew Detective King wouldn't let the Parkers get away from this investigation unscathed. She had to investigate this herself. She decided to call Amanda.

"Hey," Amanda said as she picked up the phone. She was so casual in everything she did. So casually cool, not a hint of worry in her voice, ever.

"Hey!" Sally chirped. She worried that she might be overdoing it. "I have a situation. Do you think you could help me?"

"I'm in. What's up?"

"I might have a lead on this Gina Thorpe thing. But it's my childhood best friend's husband. Can you help me figure this thing out? But we have to be really under the radar about this."

"Let's do it. Where are we going?"

"Lake Littlejohn. When is your next day off?"

"Day after tomorrow, I have the whole day off. Nicole wants to take the kids to some play. Also known as spending time with them doing something she wants to do, not something they want to do. They'll hate it, and she'll get frustrated with them. See you on Wednesday."

Chapter 9

Sally luckily had plenty of time to find a babysitter. She texted her babysitter that she preferred to use, but unfortunately, she was already busy. She didn't have many other babysitters, and far fewer that she actually liked and trusted for long periods of time. That meant she would have to ask Janice, William's mother. She called her.

"Hi Janice, it's Sally."

"Hi, dear."

"I was wondering if you could keep the baby for most of the day on Wednesday. I got a little job to help a store with inventory."

"I'd love to help, but you'll need to tell me his schedule."

"Of course, Janice. I'll write everything down for you."

Wednesday came, and Janice wanted Jackson to be at her house, which was about five minutes away. It was more difficult to pack up all his things, but Sally did it all and planned ahead because she needed the help. She told William about the fake inventory and felt guilty for lying but told herself it was for the good of her family.

She drove to Janice's house and Bruce was nowhere to be seen, probably on the golf course or fishing. Since he had retired, those were his two hobbies that took up the majority of his time.

"Thank you so much for your help today, Janice. I really appreciate it." Sally tried to sound as authentic as she could.

"You're welcome. Where is the little job that you're doing?" Sally ignored the hint of condescension in her tone.

"It's in Lake Littlejohn. I'll have my phone with me. You can call or text me with any questions or if he's having a hard time. I can come right back." She thought it important to have an aspect or detail of honesty in her story in case of an emergency. If she was in a car accident and her car was found there, she would be in a bigger mess. She said her goodbyes and headed to pick up Amanda.

She had never been to Amanda's apartment before and was surprised when it was in a nice neighborhood. She felt guilty for assuming that Amanda would live in a less-than-desirable neighborhood and then remembered that Nicole and her husband probably paid Amanda very well. Her apartment building was quaint and cute. She wondered what the inside looked like. Imagining a very eclectic aesthetic. Her vision included plants everywhere, with a dreamcatcher in the window. She texted Amanda to tell her that she had arrived and was waiting out front.

Be there soon, Amanda replied. Fifteen minutes later, Amanda stumbled out of the front door. "Sorry, sorry, sorry. I know that took too long," she said, breathless.

"It's fine, really! I was enjoying the quiet," Sally winked at her.

"What's the plan?"

"I don't have one! That's so unlike me. But I don't know what to do. I need to figure out how to find Jason or where he's staying. I just know I need to get to Lake Littlejohn. Do you have any ideas?"

"Let's think about this. We have a bit of a drive to work on a plan. Can you call Jason and say that you're in town and ask if he wants to have lunch?"

"I could, but then how do I explain your presence?"

"Good point. What about finding out where he is without him knowing?"

"That's ideal, but I don't know how to do that."

"I do."

"What do you mean? How can you do that?"

"Does he have social media?"

"Yes."

"Pull it up. I'll see what I can do."

Sally pulled up Jason's Instagram account and handed her phone to Amanda. They drove silently for nearly an hour until Amanda spoke. "Got it," she said.

"What do you mean?"

"I found the location of his latest photo. He posted a picture from a lake house where he is staying, looking out onto the lake. I found the data on the photograph and got the address. I'll type it into my GPS."

"I did not know you knew how to do that."

"One of my few high-level skills. I learned it from photography."

"Wow. Excellent. I'm glad I brought you with me," Sally said with a smile.

The two women followed the directions through the charming town of Lake Littlejohn, onto the other side of the town, and through the woods to the actual lake. They turned several times and even turned on an unmarked road to find the elusive lake house where Jason was staying. Seeing how far away from civilization the lake house was, Sally worried that they might actually find something ominous.

Why else would he stay somewhere so very far away from the courthouse? It made no sense. They spotted the house and slowly drove by, in case he was there. They did not see a car, so they turned around and doubled back to the driveway. They pulled onto the driveway and into the carport.

Sally and Amanda unbuckled their seatbelts and got out of the car. They both were moving slowly like sloths as a form of self-perseverance. They walked up to the little house and looked in the windows. It looked innocent enough, but Sally got a chill up her spine when she thought about what could await them inside. A woman's body? A woman being held hostage? The options were endless. "This way," Amanda hissed at her.

They walked around the back of the house, trying to be as stealthy as possible. There was a large deck on the back, almost as large as the house, looking out over the lake. Down the lawn there was a dock without a boat. Sally wondered if Jason had taken the boat out, but his car was gone.

The signs indicated that he was working. Underneath the deck was a little door. Sally assumed it to be a storage area. Her breath and heart rate quickened. Wordlessly the women continued toward the door and turned the knob. Locked. The bottom of the deck was a lattice design, and Sally wondered if there might be a key hidden. She reached her hand through the grates and felt around. There. Cold metal hanging on a nail. "Found it," she said.

She put the key into the lock and turned. The door loudly opened, squeaking as if it hadn't been opened in years. "Hello?" Sally said, barely more than a whisper. She realized it was nearly inaudible. "Hello?" she said a bit louder.

"Hello!" Amanda stepped in and said it loud enough to be heard. There was no response. Amanda pulled her cell phone out and tapped the flashlight function. She was starting to take the wheel on this expedition, and she barely had any ownership over what was happening, but she was invested. Sally loved her grit and tenacity and, oddly, felt safe with her, though she did not know why.

Amanda pointed the bright light at the dark room, and it came to life. Cobwebs covered almost every wall and random water toys were thrown about: a life jacket here, a raft there. She saw ancient kayaks leaning against the wall. But, no body, no woman in handcuffs, nothing. Sally let out a loud exhale.

"That was louder than when you said, 'hello,'" Amanda said with a smirk.

"I was so scared we were going to find something."

"Me too, but we're not done yet. Let's keep going."

"But--," Sally started to say but Amanda was already walking inside the storage room. Once they were both inside, Amanda started to speak again.

"I wonder if there's a way into the house through here. Like a trap door or something." Sally loved how proactive Amanda was, but she didn't think it was reasonable that there would be a trap door to the house from inside this creepy storage room, but she didn't argue. Despite Sally's protests, she understood that Amanda was going to press on.

The women walked in. The further they walked, the lower they had to crouch until they were on their hands and knees on the dirt floor. "Found it," Amanda said.

Sally was shocked and crawled over to where Amanda was. She shined her flashlight on it, showing a very small door that could be pushed to get into the main part of the house.

"Maybe not a trap door, but whatever, it works." She pushed the door, fully expecting it to be locked. It didn't budge at first, but with both of them pushing, it started to move. Slowly, it opened. The door was similar to pull-down steps that go into an attic but reverse for a basement. It was rusty and needed to be oiled, but it worked.

They only needed to use one of the steps to get inside the house. Amanda went in first, to the surprise of no one. "Come on," she said, pulling Sally up. They stepped on the linoleum kitchen floor and looked around. The kitchen was dated but workable. It was what Sally expected based on the outside of the home. It looked like it had last been updated in the eighties, and even then, not to a high level of quality. The white refrigerator was yellowing and peeling, and the faux wood countertops were popping up in some places. But again, no missing woman, no body.

They walked through the kitchen into the entirely wood-paneled living room. One fading dark plaid recliner sat angled towards an aging brown leather couch. In between those was a tan coffee table that showed years of wear in the countless rings on its surface. Behind the sofa was a narrow hallway which the women followed to the one and only bedroom. The bedroom was basic and practical, like the rest of the house, only housing a metal framed bed covered with a quilt, a wooden bedside table, and one chair for seating.

The bag that Sally could only assume was Jason's sat on the chair. There was only one other room to search, the bathroom at the end of the hall, past the bedroom. There was no closet. Jason had hung his suits from the ceiling fan. They had all but seen the bathroom already because it was so small, and they could see in it as they walked down the hall.

Quiet, wordlessly, they moved to search it. A small shower, pedestal sink, and toilet were all that occupied the room. In order to check all the boxes, Sally opened the frosted door to the shower to make sure a woman was not inside. And she wasn't. Thank God, she thought. But a feeling of disappointment overwhelmed the pit of her stomach. If Gina isn't here, she thought, then where is she?

"Well, I guess she isn't here," Amanda said.

"Let's get out of here," Sally replied. "This place gives me the creeps."

As they walked back through the house and through the kitchen, Sally saw something out of the corner of her eye. As she looked through the kitchen window, her eyes suddenly met with Jason's.

She thought about running, but he had seen her. The look in his eyes was one of confusion and alarm. Of course, it was. There was no explanation for why she would be inside his rental house in this strange town. "Oh my God, Jason," she said and looked at Amanda. Amanda's eyes filled with fear. "It will be fine. I've got this." Sally said, feigning confidence.

Jason opened the door. "Sally... what are you doing here? Inside my rental? Is Kat okay?" He looked genuinely confused and concerned.

"Jason, let me explain. Kat is fine. First, this is my friend Amanda." She said as her brain whizzed and flitted, trying to think of a reasonable explanation. Her shoulders drooped as she knew there was no explanation, and he was probably already figuring it out.

"Good. So why are you here?" He was starting to look angry.

"Jason, you know what's been going on with me, right? I mean, William said he told you, and I'm sure Kat told you as well."

"Yes. I'm going to ask you one more time," he said as he took an intrusive step forward, "Sally, why are you here?" Both women instinctively took a step back.

"The last place Gina Thorpe's credit card was used was here, in Lake Littlejohn. And you're here. So, I wanted to come and see if I could find her."

"In my rental?" Jason's voice was now beginning to rise, and redness was surging out from his crisp, clean white button-down.

"I'm sorry. I'm really sorry. I'm just trying to protect my family."

"By suspecting me?!" His voice boomed, reaching every corner of the small room.

"Sorry, but we were just trying to cross our t's and dot our i's," Amanda added, trying to diffuse the situation, but it didn't work.

"Shut up," Jason demanded of her, and she took another step back. This time she was almost entirely behind Sally. Sally had become her armor.

"Jason, okay. We're leaving, I'm sorry. I'm just trying to figure out what's going on here."

"Anything else you want to take before you go? A swab of my DNA?" He said sarcastically, his arms raised in the air as if the police had said, "Put your hands up." The women made themselves small to slide past him and out the door.

Sally slid into the driver's seat and put the key in the ignition the exact moment she put the car in drive. "Buckle up," she said to Amanda, and they drove silently through the woods back to the main road.

After nearly ten minutes of driving, Amanda spoke. "Well, that didn't go well."

"I am in such a big steaming pile of trouble right now, Amanda. You don't even know. William and Katherine are both going to kill me. I'm so sorry I brought you into this with me."

"Are you kidding? That was exciting!" Amanda said.

"It was, wasn't it?" Sally laughed.

"But aside from that awful confrontation, let's think about the facts," Amanda said. "Now we know Gina isn't there. So that's one thing we can mark off the list."

"That's true. I still feel like I can figure this out. I know that sounds crazy. I can't tell anyone but you that, but I really feel like I can."

"I think you can, too," said Amanda. They sat quietly the rest of the way home. The only sound between them the humming of their brains in tune, working together, trying to solve a crime.

Chapter 10

Sally went to pick up Jackson from Janice and took a deep breath to change her demeanor. She was worried, scared, and confused; she felt out of control. She was waiting for a call from Katherine and William, but she hadn't gotten that yet. Maybe Jason wouldn't tell them, but she knew better than that. She knocked on the door of Janice and Bruce's brick home before letting herself in.

"Hi, sweet boy!" she said as she scooped up her little boy. She meant what she said. "How did he do?"

"He was great," Janice said. "We had fun." She wasn't overly enthusiastic in general, and there was no change in her behavior when children were involved. It explained her husband's lack of enthusiasm.

"I'm so glad. I missed you, buddy!"

"How was your work trip?" Janice asked. She didn't usually ask about Sally's work. Sally wasn't sure, but she always got the idea that Janice didn't like that

Sally still worked part-time. Janice never worked. Sally assumed Janice expected the same of her. But Sally liked having something to stimulate her brain when she wasn't underwater with play dates, bottles, and diapers.

"It was great! Thanks for asking." Sally rounded up all of Jackson's things one-handed because she was holding him. A skilled technique. They left, saying their goodbyes and thank yous to Janice. Bruce was still nowhere to be seen, which was fine with Sally because he wasn't engaged with Jackson even when he was around. She wondered if he even knew Jackson's middle name.

On the drive home, Sally decided to pretend like everything was fine until she was confronted with the truth of what had happened that day. She had come up with a plan. It was what she did best: plan. She had learned to plan when she was a child. Her parents never had a plan. Some might call them hippies, but they were no-doubt free spirits.

They lived life one moment to the next. Nothing wrong with that, but difficult for a young child who needs information and stability to thrive. Sally began to make these plans for her family. Her parents were agreeable and understanding that this was what she needed. They still didn't make plans. Instead, they allowed her to take the driver's seat and would follow along with her.

Her plan for today was simple. Act normal. Do not be suspicious. Text Kat tonight and ask her to have lunch tomorrow in the hope that Jason didn't tell her anything. She silently wished and prayed all night that everything would be fine and that no one would be angry with her. Along with being a planner, Sally was a pacifist; knowing that someone was angry with her was like a cancer, a disease that ate away at her from the inside out.

All night Sally tossed and turned. She constantly checked the monitor to make sure Jackson was safe. With all of these goings on with Gina missing and possibly murdered, Sally became consumed with anxiety that someone would take Jackson from his bed without her knowing. Each time she rolled over, she wished for things to go back to the way they were, for this all to be a dream.

Morning came and as she opened her eyes, Sally knew it wasn't a dream. She checked her phone and Katherine had texted her that she could meet up for lunch. A familiar pang in her stomach welcomed her to the new day. She knew she would have to put her big girl pants on and face whatever retribution was coming her way.

She still secretly and silently hoped that Jason hadn't told Kat what had happened. She was sure there were plenty of other things he never told her. Sally had her suspicions that Jason had been entrenched in at least one affair, based on what Katherine had told her; he had stories that didn't add up, at least to Sally.

Sally left Jackson with the babysitter and bravely went on her way to meet up with Katherine. They were going to have lunch and Sally was no longer anxious. She was afraid. She would know what Katherine would say as soon as their eyes met. Sally parked her car and steeled herself to endure this encounter.

Sally scanned the dining room of the restaurant with her eyes finally landing on Katherine in a corner booth, difficult to find. Katherine looked at her wordlessly, no smile passing her lips. She knew. Sally walked over to the booth feeling as if she were moving in slow motion, walking to the gallows of her longest friendship.

"Hi, Kat," Sally said, sliding into the booth.

"Really? Hi? That's all you're going to say?"

"I know you're upset."

"No, Sally. Upset is what I was last week when I thought you were a little unhinged. Upset is not what I am right now. What I am right now is furious." She emphasized the word "furious" as the little vein on the side of her head popped out. Sally had seen that vein pop plenty of times, but never towards or about her.

"I'm sorry. I was wrong to suspect Jason," Sally said as her voice cracked, holding back tears.

"Don't even think about crying or trying to play the victim here, Sally. What is going on with you? You broke into my husband's rental because you thought he was holding a missing woman hostage? This is insane."

"I know. I know! It's driving me nuts. I'm just trying to solve this." Sally said as she looked up. She saw a waiter coming towards their table and then, seeing the heat of their conversation, turned to another table entirely.

"I'm going to stop you right there. It isn't your job to solve this. You realize that, right? You aren't a police officer. You aren't an investigative journalist. You aren't any of those things. You are not involved in this at all. You made all of this chaos happen yourself."

Sally thought about her words. Had she brought all of this upon herself? She didn't think so, but maybe Katherine was right. Perhaps she was so bored and unfulfilled that she had gone out searching for something to consume her time without even realizing it. But she didn't think. That purse jumped out at her for a reason that she did not yet understand. She physically shook her head.

"Why are you shaking your head? Do I need to have you committed? Do I need to call William? Because I swear to God, Sally, I'm close to doing both of those things. You're scaring me." The warmth returned to her voice and Sally could tell she was worried about her. She knew the anger was more hurt than hatred.

"I'm sorry, Katherine. Really, I am. I am trying really hard to figure out what's going on here because I think there's a reason I found that purse. I know going into Jason's rental was wrong. I'm afraid if I don't find Gina or at least find some sort of big clue, Detective King is going to try to pin this crime on me, William, or worse, both of us."

"You're very lucky Jason isn't going to press charges for breaking and entering. I had to talk him out of it."

"Thank you very much for doing that. He never liked me anyway."

"He did like you... before this." Katherine said. But Sally knew that Jason didn't like her, and the feeling was mutual. There was always an air of displeasure between the two of them. Jason thought Sally was controlling and manipulating Katherine, and Sally thought Katherine could do better. Everyone knew the feelings that lingered between the two of them, yet Katherine never said a word about it. Maybe the heaviness between them was not apparent to her.

The two women sat and stared at each other, unsure how to move forward from this. This large, awkward iceberg between them. Sally broke the uncomfortable silence.

"I hope one day you'll be able to forgive me."

"I'll work on it," Katherine said. With that, Sally got up and went to her car without ever ordering or eating a meal. Their lunch date was more of a neutral place to meet and hash it out. She went to her car and began to drive. She expected the tears to come, yet they didn't. She was ready for war. Ready to fight. The old Sally was gone. The new Sally put on her armor.

Chapter 11

Sally dialed Amanda's phone. "Hello?" she said. "Hey. I just saw Katherine. Jason told her. I don't think she mentioned you, though."

"Thank God. No offense, but I don't need people hating me as much as they hate you right now."

"What do you mean? People know about this?"

"I heard Nicole talking about you on the phone."

"Oh, God. What was she saying?"

"She said she heard that you were under suspicion for whatever was going on with Gina Thorpe."

"How does she even know about that?"

"I have no idea, but I want to stay off her radar."

"Understood. Katherine told me she had to talk Jason out of pressing charges. Which is ridiculous because I think he's a big fat cheater, but whatever, Jason." Sally whined.

"Are you still looking for clues?"

"Definitely still looking. I have yet to hear from Detective King, but I got the picture that he was not going to stop going after me until he found a way to prove that I'm involved. Which for the record, I'm not. But I think someone is trying to pin this on me."

"Obviously."

"I have to figure out why." It was clear the conversation was over, and Sally hung up the phone without saying goodbye. She knew Amanda wouldn't mind. She didn't take things personally like Sally's few other friends. Sally loved that about her.

Sally drove home, hopeful that Jackson would be down for a nap when she arrived. She was out of luck when she pulled into the driveway and saw him playing in the front yard with the babysitter, who had tried to put him down without success.

The job was now Sally's. She didn't mind. Nap time with him was her favorite. Bedtime was another story. She couldn't understand why she enjoyed one and not the other.

Following putting Jackson down for his nap, her phone buzzed. She looked and saw a phone number that she was once unfamiliar with, but now she knew. The police station. Detective King. She knew not to answer. William's familiar words of not talking to the police without a lawyer present rang in her head.

She was reminded that she had not told William about the encounter with Jason, and didn't plan to, yet she wondered if this was a poor choice. William was high justice, and he would never forgive her if he knew she was lying to him. She didn't see it as lying, but she knew he would.

As if on cue, her phone rang. It was William. "Guess who just called me," she answered the phone with a question.

"Who?"

"Detective King. I didn't answer."

"Maybe you should have. I just talked to Jason." Sally's stomach dropped. She didn't expect Jason to be such a tattletale.

"William, I can explain."

"Sally, don't. First, you think I'm having an affair. Now you're breaking and entering into Jason's rented house?"

"Why does everyone keep saying that? Breaking and entering?"

"Who is everyone?" William said with anger creeping into his voice.

"Katherine. Jason told her as well. But I'll tell you what happened. Detective King told me that the last place Gina Thorpe's credit card was used was in Lake Littlejohn. Then Kat told me Jason had a trial there. So, I went to see if something was going on there. It seemed like too much of a coincidence. Did I do the wrong thing? Absolutely. Am I terrified that Detective King will find a way to pin this missing person and/or murder on us? Yes. Now I know Jason is not involved. Katherine is furious at me, as is Jason. I don't blame either of them. But, William, I am trying to protect us."

"Alright, Sally. I get it. But couldn't you at least have told me first? Why lie?"

"Because I knew you would tell me not to go, not to do it."

"You're right. I would have said that."

"I had to go and find out what was going on for myself. Detective King has made it very clear that he has one person, or persons, in mind for this crime. If he isn't going to do his job to figure out what has happened to this poor woman, I will. If not for her, then for Jackson. Do you understand what I'm saying, William?"

"I understand. But make me a promise, will you?"

"What is it?" She didn't want to make a promise she couldn't keep.

"Next time, be honest with me. Please. Just tell me."

"I can make that promise. Next time I will tell you the truth. If you can promise me that you won't absolutely lose your mind and tell me no."

"I think these are both promises we can keep," William said, and Sally could hear the smile cross his lips through the phone. They wordlessly hung up. Sally was pleasantly surprised with how William took the news of her vigilante justice. He had certainly taken it a lot better than Katherine, but it had affected Katherine more inherently. She understood that and didn't resent Kat for being angry with her. She only hoped that Katherine would be able to forgive her and that their friendship would be restored to its original brass.

Following her conversation with William, Sally checked on Jackson on the monitor to ensure his safety. Safe and sound, she thought as she watched him sleep in his crib. She walked to the mailbox and gathered the mail, having seen it being dropped off as she was on the phone with William.

She carried it inside and laid it on the counter. Busying herself with other tasks: dishes, laundry, wiping down the countertops until she realized she had forgotten to sort through it. She grabbed the catalogs she wouldn't read and placed them in a pile for the recycling bin.

She sorted through the bills and found a plain white, unmarked envelope with only the word "SALLY," typed in a basic typewriter font. She opened it and unfolded the paper that was inside. Her hands began to shake as she read the words, "STOP DIGGING."

She dropped the paper and it floated slowly to the ground, left and right, as the overhead fan made it swing and sway this way and that. The words stunned her. She was afraid.

She wasn't paranoid. There was a real threat. She looked around to see if she was being watched. Yet, she was alone in her house. She went to the front door and pulled the blinds back to look out... no one was there.

Her shaking hands began to slow, and she knew what she must do. She must press on and solve the crime. Because this was more than a rumor now. Someone knew what she knew. They knew that Sally was being implicated and that she was starting to unravel what was really going on with Gina Thorpe.

She would solve this crime, even if she had to do it alone.

Chapter 12

Sally knew there was one person, and one person only, who she could tell about the letter she received: Amanda. She called her because she didn't want a record of her sending the message on her phone.

"Hello?"

"Hey. You won't believe what just happened." Sally said.

"You solved it?" Amanda asked enthusiastically.

"Not yet, but I'm getting there. I got an anonymous letter in my mailbox that said, 'Stop digging.'"

"Oh my God," Amanda sounded shocked as she said the words and gasped simultaneously.

"I know," Sally said, "someone knows what I'm up to, and I think they're willing to do anything to make me stop. Don't ask me how I'm handling this because my anxiety is on another level. I'm so worried that someone will try to take Jackson."

"I don't want to make you worry more, but that's a valid fear based on what we've seen and what we know," Amanda said. "So, what's next?"

"I'm not sure, but I'll keep you in the loop... whatever happens." Sally hung up the phone without so much as a goodbye.

Her mind had not stopped swirling since her and Amanda's encounter with Jason, and she knew it wouldn't stop anytime soon. Her main goal was to keep Jackson safe, yet nothing felt safe. Someone had been watching her. That much was clear. If someone was watching her, then it meant they were watching Jackson and possibly William as well.

The thought of being watched and followed made her feel even more paranoid. Yet, she wasn't paranoid. She was aware. Aware of the reality of her circumstances. And aware that her child was in genuine danger. If the person who did this to Gina knew Sally was digging, which they obviously did, then what would they be willing to do to try and stop her? She couldn't take her eyes off of the baby monitor.

Knowing that Jackson was safe was her only tether to reality, keeping her feet on the ground. She peeled herself away only to pull back the curtains on the front of their home again to see if she saw anyone: nothing.

She gets an idea and texts Amanda: "Want to see if we can get inside her house?" She knows it sounds crazy, but it might just work. First, she needs to find out where Gina Thorpe lives. Then she can figure out how to get inside, one step at a time.

Amanda texts back: "Let's do it."

Sally's adrenaline starts to rush again, and she feels inspired and invigorated. No one is going to stop her from finding out what happened to Gina. She reminds herself that she found the purse for a reason. This isn't a coincidence. Gina has no one on her side, if she's even still alive, and Sally is going to try her hardest to help her.

Sally pulls open her computer and opens the public records website to find Gina's address. She searches to no avail. She wonders if Gina is short for something. She tries her search again, this time using the name Regina. Bingo. Found it. And wouldn't you know it... She lived in the same apartment complex as Amanda. Different building, same property.

Sally picks up the phone to call Amanda again. "You won't believe our luck."

"What happened?" Amanda asks.

"She lived in the same apartment complex as you."

"You're kidding."

"Serious as a heart attack," Sally says.

"You're about to give me one. I never saw any police or anything around here. Don't you find that odd?"

"Your apartment complex is big, I wouldn't expect you to see them. And they're probably trying to keep it as quiet as possible because they don't want single women like you, to freak out and break their lease and move."

"True."

"Now- how are we going to get in her apartment?"

"Let me handle that. Come over tomorrow at noon." Amanda says.

"See you then."

Click.

The time for Jackson to start his first Mother's Day Out program couldn't have come at a better or worse time. Sally needed him to be somewhere else so she could try to solve this crime, but she also felt extreme unease that something would happen to him while she was gone; or worse, someone would take him while she was gone. But still, she had put him on a waitlist for a highly regarded Mother's Day Out, and he had finally gotten in. She took him on his first day, which was also the day that Sally and Amanda were going to attempt to search Gina's apartment- it was a big day for everyone. Sally tried her tears from drop-off and pulled into the apartment complex. Surprisingly, Amanda ran out the moment Sally pulled up. She opened the door and didn't speak until it was closed.

"She lived in that building right over there," Amanda pointed as she spoke. "I'm so freaked out that she lived so close to me. I mean, it could have been me...."

"No, it couldn't. I'm convinced this wasn't random." Sally felt strong and powerful with her words as she eased Amanda's mind. Sally could feel herself growing from the inside out during this experience, and she didn't want to go back to the wallflower she once was. She pulled the car around the corner, easing from one parking lot to another.

"Now, how are we going to get in her apartment?" Sally asked.

"I told you I would handle it," Amanda said with a smirk. "The maintenance guy and I smoke weed together," she said with a snorting laugh, "and I think he has a crush on me. So I texted him and asked if we could meet up and we hung out last night. I asked him if he would help us, and he said yes. So, he's waiting on us with a key." She winked as she said it.

"Wow," Sally said, "you're good."

Sally parked the car, and they got out. The maintenance guy, with a nametag that said Jake, was waiting underneath the awning. His face lit up when he saw Amanda. Poor guy thought Sally.

"Thanks for helping us out!" Amanda said perkily.

"No problem. This one, right?"

"Right!"

Jake unlocked the door and let them in. It was a small two-bedroom, but nice. The apartment was clean, and she had decorated it in a mix of whites and pastels. Sally felt even more connected to Gina at this moment. It felt intimate. She was in Gina's space, possibly the space where she was taken.

The gravity of the moment caught in Sally's throat. She swallowed and got back down to business. She had work to do. She scanned the living room and kitchen for anything out of the ordinary. Immediately she saw the silver glint of Gina's laptop. She felt pulled to it, like a magnet. She wonders why the police didn't have her laptop in custody and what else they may have missed.

It seems like they either don't know how to or don't want to do their jobs. A woman with zero police training is closer to the truth than they are. Are they bumbling this investigation on purpose? Sally doesn't have time to think about this now. She bookmarks it in her mind and swiftly opens the laptop. It comes to life and requests a password. She looks up, aware that others are in the room with her for the first time since they entered.

"Jake, you wouldn't happen to be a hacker, would you?" she asks.

"No...." he says.

"I knew we couldn't get that lucky," Sally sighs.

She closes the laptop temporarily and walks around the apartment to see what else she can find that might be a clue. She opens drawers in the kitchen and finds nothing of note; a junk drawer, silverware, and dishtowels. She meanders into Gina's bedroom, and it seems like a moment frozen in time.

It is untouched and clean. As if Gina expected to come home and crawl into bed and go on living her life. Yet that didn't happen. Something happened, but what? She was taken. She was killed. She is being held hostage somewhere. She is being trafficked. The options are endless, each possibility more disturbing than the last.

She looks under Gina's bed, in her closet, and in her bathroom and finds nothing. She walks into the other bedroom, which Gina has turned into a guest bedroom slash office with a white lacquer desk and filing cabinet underneath. She shuffles the papers on the desk and sees real estate contracts, notes with addresses, and shreds of paper with what she assumes are client requests. *Four bedroom downtown with a yard. Two-bedroom apartment with pool. Three bedroom in Westlake school district.*

She opens the file cabinet and immediately sees a red envelope. She opens it and sees a note written on heavy cardstock with a small gold bird at the top; Sally knows this is expensive stationary. It reads: *I love you, my darling. Happy Valentine's Day. I promise our next one will be just the two of us, and I vow to make things less complicated for us. I'll fix this. XO*

Sally stuffs the note back in the envelope and shoves it in her bag. She doesn't recognize the handwriting, but that doesn't mean anything other than William didn't write the note, which is a relief to her. She quickly walks back to the kitchen and living room area and finds Amanda.

"Let's go," she says.

"Did you find anything?" Amanda asks.

"Let's go to your place, and I'll tell you." She doesn't want Jake to hear anything she has to say.

"Okay. Bye, Jake. Thanks for your help!"

They walk to the building that is Amanda's and go inside her apartment. The floorplan is the same as Gina's, but smaller, one bedroom instead of two. It is not what Sally expected. It is clean, minimalist, with only a small area of the living reserved for art. Sally realizes

Amanda doesn't have many things. They sit down at the kitchen table.

"So, what did you find?" Amanda asks in anticipation.

"I found a note from her lover. Here," Sally grabs the note and hands it to Amanda. "What do you think it means? Tell me your ideas, and I'll tell you mine."

"Hmmm," Amanda says while she reads it. "Sounds to me like she was having an affair with a married man, possibly with children?" She says it like a question.

"My thoughts exactly," Sally says. "Now the question... Who? I don't know anything about the stationary, but I know that the handwriting isn't William's. Thank God."

Chapter 13

Sally picks Jackson up from Mother's Day Out, and he is fussy and tired from his first day. His teacher said he wouldn't nap, so she knows that means an early bedtime for him. They get home, and she gets him a snack and lets him watch a show, so she can think more about the note she found at Gina's apartment.

She opens Facebook and pulls up Gina's profile. Next, she opens Gina's friends' list, scans it, and sees nothing of note. Then, she clicks on their mutual friends, and there are no men. She swipes out of Facebook with a sigh. She feels like she's at another dead end. Her phone comes back to life with a phone call from Katherine. Her stomach drops seeing her name, wondering if she is still upset with her.

"Hello?" she answers with trepidation.

"Have you seen the news?" Katherine says.

"No. What's going on?"

"Turn it on and call me back." Click.

With shaking hands, Sally turns on the local news. There is an anchor on the screen broadcasting on a bridge. Below the anchor is a flashing headline: **BODY FOUND IN RIVER BELIEVED TO BE MISSING WOMAN, GINA THORPE.**

Sally gasped and dropped the television remote control. The room feels like it is spinning, and she feels unable to grasp reality. She looks over at Jackson eating his snack and lining up his trucks. She begins to settle back in. Suddenly Detective King comes on the screen, "We cannot confirm or deny the findings today. After identifying the body, we will alert the public. Thank you." He speaks in his trademark gravelly monotone voice. With shaky hands, Sally grabs her phone and calls Katherine back.

"I can't believe this," she says, almost in tears.

"I know. I knew this would be hard for you. Are you okay?"

"I'm not sure. I knew something like this had happened."

"We all suspected it, but knowing it's real feels... heavier."

"I have to help her. I have to find out who did this to her."

"I know you do. Just please, Sally, please be careful. This is getting very dangerous. For all of us."

"I know. I will. Talk soon." Sally hung up the phone.

Sally did a quick Google search for the news headline and texted it to William and then to Amanda. It hadn't been confirmed yet, that was true, but everyone knew. Gina had been missing for weeks. It was obvious that she had been murdered. *Murdered*. The word stirred the bile in Sally's stomach. How could this have happened to this woman? She thought an affair was no reason to kill someone. Killed. Murdered. Her life taken. Her breath caught in her throat as she thought of Gina's body, cold and bloated, floating in the river.

She ran to the bathroom and coughed up the contents of her stomach into the toilet. She was sick.

With fear, dread, sadness, and anger. She didn't want to be involved in this horrible situation, and yet she was. No one else seemed to care about Gina except Sally. She looked in the mirror at her red face and tear-stained eyes and promised to fight for Gina. Justice for Gina. She didn't know what that looked like, but she would fight for it.

William comes through the door like a cannonball. Sally didn't even know he was coming home. He goes to her like a magnet, and their bodies meet with arms going where they belong, fitting like a puzzle. She falls into him, sobbing, thankful that Jackson is too young to understand what's happening.

She weeps for her past, her future, but mostly for Gina. Gina. A woman she had never met, yet she cries for Gina. Gina will never know a moment like this: pure agony being caught by the one who loves you. Gina was betrayed by the one she loved or someone close to her. Sally cries for who-knows-how-long and takes a deep gasping breath bringing her back to reality, like she is swimming and coming up for air. In her own way, she is doing just that. She looks up at William, and they finally speak.

"I'm so sorry," he says. As if Sally had lost a family member of her own.

"Me too," she says.

Suddenly, the doorbell rings. Jackson waddles over to look out the front door and see who it is. William and Sally walk hand-in-hand to answer it together. They move in unison. Sally takes a deep breath when she realizes who it is: Detective King.

She knows it isn't good if he's coming to their home. Sally and William glance at one another and steel themselves for what's to come. Sally is relieved to know she has, at least, William on her team. William opens the door, "Detective King, to what do I owe the pleasure?" William is skilled at being kind and condescending at the same time.

"May I come in?" Detective King asks.
This time he has an air of kindness and respect.

"Of course. Come in." Sally says.

They take a seat on the sofa and pair of chairs in the living room. "This is our son, Jackson. Can you say 'hi' to Detective King?" Sally says. Jackson doesn't say hello but instead goes to find a different truck. This time he wants his garbage truck.

"Hi, bud," Detective King says. "Listen, I didn't want to talk to you all in front of a kid, but I guess we don't have much of a choice, do we?"

"When you come to our home, our son is here," William says.

"Understood," Detective King says, "I'm sure you've seen the news by now. And we just got the word that we can confirm that the body is that of Gina Thorpe."

"Oh my God," Sally says and throws herself into William's chest.

"It's not how we wanted this thing to go, that's for sure. But we suspected this would be the case, given how long she's been missing. We've seen it before, and we'll see it again, unfortunately." He clears his throat. "But that's not why I'm here."

"Then why are you here?" William asks. He is not the least bit intimidated by Detective King. He has always been confident in business, and that carries over to any kind of meeting. Sally is beyond relieved that he is here with her.

"Sally. We heard from a reputable source that you searched Gina's apartment. Is that true?"

"Yes," Sally doesn't even bother lying or making an excuse. She is too exhausted.

"I've told you before, and I'll tell you again right now... Stay out of this investigation. This is now a homicide investigation, and I can tell you that the likes of you two don't want to get involved in a homicide investigation. This is serious stuff. Stay in your lane." He says the last sentence as if there is punctuation between each word.

"I understand where you're coming from, Detective King. This is your job, not mine. However, at the time, I did feel like the work was not being done to find Gina and find out what happened to her."

"Just because it looks like I'm not doing my job from a public perspective does not mean I'm not doing it. I came here as a courtesy. Stay out of this investigation, or I will have you charged with obstruction of justice."

"We understand. Thank you for the information and for coming. I'll see you out." William says as he gets up. He acts as if he knows everything Detective King is talking about. He shuts the door and calmly walks back to Sally.

"What did we say about keeping secrets?" he asks, and Sally feels like a child.

"It happened today. I didn't even get a chance to tell you."

"Wow, he's really on top of it then."

"On top of everything except solving this murder."

"Sally—"

"I know, I know. Stay in my lane." She says with a sigh.

Chapter 14

The next several days are up and down with internal conflict for Sally. She wonders if she should "stay in her lane" or if she is the only one who truly has the tools to solve Gina's murder. She doesn't know how Gina was killed and, truthfully, doesn't know if she wants to find out. She is too close, and though she never met Gina, she feels like she did.

She has texted with Amanda but not at length, so she decides to see if she wants to meet up after her accounting work. She elects to ask William's mother, Janice, if she can babysit Jackson for the afternoon so she can get her work done. Janice doesn't need to know she is also having lunch with a friend. Technically, it's a working lunch. She knows she and Amanda will discuss Gina's murder.

Again, Sally decides to refrain from discussing anything via text message with Amanda. She knows that once it's in writing, it is traceable and etched in time and space forever. She drops Jackson off with Janice. Down the hall, she can see her father-in-law, Bruce, working in his office.

She doesn't know what kind of work he does since he's retired, but everyone is content leaving him to his devices in his dark office. Everything in his office is dark oak and leather and smells of a faint hint of cigars, even though he assures Janice he doesn't smoke them. The walls are adorned with built-in cabinets with ornate trim, and his oversized desk sits in the middle of the room. There is no computer, scanner, or printer.

The only technology on his desk is an old office telephone with many buttons for each line. At this office, there are only two lines, one for "business" and one for their personal telephone. It mimics the phones in the office he spent every day for forty years.

She makes a note to ask William what Bruce actually does, though she assumes it's some type of consulting because it seems that's what every retired old man does before he can fully take work off the table. He was a banker and looks every bit the part.

He doesn't know how to dress down, loves a suit, and speaks eloquently. The only time Sally sees him is when she peeks into his office or if he is watching television on the couch as she enters. He's always nice but never engaged in any way.

Sally kisses Jackson goodbye, and Janice seems genuinely excited to spend the day with him. Sally's heart swells thinking of her sweet baby boy and all that she is willing to do to protect him. That's what all of this is about, Sally's maternal instinct. Gina was once someone's baby. That triggers her mind to think of Gina's memorial. She hasn't seen anything in the news about it, but surely it will be happening soon. Unless they still have her body in the crime laboratory. The thought makes Sally feel sick. Again, she feels like she must do the work to find out what happened to Gina because she feels that no one else will.

Sally works in the back office of the boutique for two hours before she gets her spreadsheets just the way she likes them. She tells the owner that she's done and that she'll invoice her. This work used to be her bread and butter, but now it's an afterthought. Sally has more important work to attend to. She left and texted Amanda that she was on her way to the restaurant.

Sally pulls up to the restaurant and sees Amanda's Subaru in the parking lot. She goes in to find her in a booth in the back, which helps Sally relax.

"Hey," Sally greets Amanda with a smile.

"Let's get into it," Amanda says, never one to engage in small talk.

"Right. So you know that she was murdered."

"Yep," Amanda says. "What else do you know?"

"Nothing really at this point. I haven't heard any details, but Detective King did drop by my house right after they found her body and told me to, and I quote, 'stay in my lane.'"

"Wow. That guy really has it out for you."

"I know. But I was thinking, I wonder when her memorial service will be."

"Who knows. I mean, is her body even at a funeral home?" Amanda asks.

"I don't know. I was thinking the same thing. Do you know anyone who works at the crime lab? Ugh, even saying that makes me feel sick to my stomach."

"Nope, I don't."

"I knew it couldn't be that easy," Sally tells her.

As luck would have it, the very next day, Gina's obituary pops up in the paper. Sally used to love reading the obituaries to find unique ones and love stories of decades past, but she no longer enjoys them since this has unfolded. She now scans them just to see Gina's.

The picture makes Gina look bright and alive, unlike how she must have been found floating in the river. How could the light have gone out of her eyes so quickly, as if in a blink? Sally couldn't bear to read the details of her life. She thought about Gina's parents sitting down to write their daughter's obituary, and the idea made the bile in her stomach churn. She thought of her own child, Jackson, and a vision flashed in her head of her and William sitting down at their kitchen table to write his obituary.

She quickly swipes that image from her mind and scans Gina's real obituary to see when her memorial service is. Ah, two days from now, Saturday. 10 am. She pulls out her phone to text Amanda. She finds herself texting Amanda much more than Kat lately. She worries that she and Kat will always feel disconnected after what happened with Jason.

Sally: *Have you seen the paper? Obituary.*

Amanda: *Just pulled it up as you texted. Saw the memorial. Are you going*

Sally: *I'm not sure. What do you think?*

Amanda: *You'll look guilty if you don't go, and guilty if you do go. So I say fuck it, go.*

Sally: *Lol, I like your logic. Will you go with me?*

Amanda: *Duh.*

Sally feels guilty about feeling excited about Gina's memorial. She thinks of all the things she will need to look for while there: people who might be guilty; Gina's family members; single men alone; police officers, etc. She also wonders what to wear and then reminds herself, this isn't about me. She decides to discuss her attendance with William, whom she knows will take issue with the matter. That evening when they are watching their television show, she brings it up.

"William, did you see the paper today?"

"You know I never read the paper. Why?"

"Gina Thorpe's obituary was in there today."

"Oh."

"I know. It said when her memorial service is as well..." Sally said as her voice trailed off.

"Don't tell me you're thinking of going."

"I'm not thinking about it. I'm going."

"Sally! What are you thinking?" William pauses the television.

"I know, William. I knew you wouldn't be happy about this."

"What did you expect me to say? Good luck? You are continuing this destructive pattern, Sally. You are risking it all for a woman you have never met. I cannot continue to support this. I forbid you to go."

"Forbid me? Forbid me?! Who do you think you are, my father?" The air comes out of the room when Sally says this. She knows there's no turning back from this argument.

"I will no longer be privy to your unreasonable and ridiculous plans to derail our family."

"I'm not trying to derail our family, William. I'm trying to solve a murder. You know, a murder that no one else seems interested in solving? You might remember." Sally surprises even herself with her aggression.

"I can't deal with this, Sally. I'm going to go stay at my parents' house tonight."

"You've got to be kidding me. Are you serious?"

"Yes, I am."

"William, wait—" Sally says, but it's too late. He's already gone.

Chapter 15

Sally faces the impossible choice of being pulled toward her family and her ethical obligation. For some women, it's work or staying home to raise their family. For others, it's doing what you feel you must do versus what you feel you should.

A modern-day war being fought daily in the homes and minds of women everywhere- with no right answer and an argument for each approach, women must make the painful choice each day. Something to be lost either way, a battle to be fought, yet we press on and do what we must. For Sally, that means moving forward with finding out what happened to Gina.

She does not feel this is a choice. It is a magnetic pull, a moral commitment, her responsibility. Not only for Gina's, but also for her family. She can't help feeling that her family is in danger either way, whether she pursues this or not. And she will not let anything happen to them.

Sally showers, dries her hair, curls it, puts on makeup, and pulls on her most tasteful black dress. She wants to fit in and disappear in the crowd. Surely this will do it. She will look like just another one of Gina's friends, albeit a bit older. But she and Amanda are friends, and they are years apart in age. The thought strikes her that she might look like a friend supporting Amanda in the crowd. Yes, she is hopeful this will be the narrative.

Sally drops Jackson off at Janice and Bruce's home, now the current home of William, and they barely speak a word. She doesn't have to say where she's going, and he doesn't ask.

She realizes that she has become more independent and stronger since everything began with the pink purse, and she has Gina to thank for that. The least of all she can do in return for Gina is go to her memorial. She drives to Amanda's and picks her up. Amanda looks lovely in a floor-length black dress. Sally realizes she has never seen Amanda in a dress.

"I love your dress," she says as Amanda opens the door and lightly sits in the seat. She seems gentler today.

"Thanks. Are you nervous?"

"Yes. But I have to tell you. William left last night."

"What?!" Amanda asks in a higher tone.

"I know. He said he couldn't deal with me trying to solve this murder and that I was putting my family in jeopardy," Sally said with an eye roll. He doesn't understand. She has a mother's instinct.

"Wow, what a dick."

"Amanda!"

"Sorry, but he needs to get it together."

"I agree."

"I'm nervous about going to this memorial. I know you are too. But I haven't been to a church since I was a kid," Amanda says.

"Really?" Sally says more as a statement than a question. She doesn't want to pry or force Amanda to share because she knows religion can be a touchy subject for almost everyone.

"Yeah, my grandparents were obsessed with going to church, like more obsessed with church than us. My parents stopped going for some reason, and we had this big falling out. I never saw my grandparents again."

"Wow, that sounds traumatic," Sally says, but she is losing interest. She is more interested in where they are going.

They pull up to the church, and men and women are already filing in. Sally notices there are no children, but why would there be? Gina didn't have children. Sally's stomach lurches as she remembers that Gina will never be able to have children. You can't have children when you're dead. The thought steels her mind for what she's here to do- spot a possible perpetrator.

Amanda and Sally nonchalantly file into the church and find a seat. They arrived early, but already there are only a few seats left. Sally knows this will be a standing-room-only event. If not for showing who Gina was as a person, then for the sheer shock factor of the "Missing and Murdered" storyline. Surely there will be people here who didn't even know Gina. *Like you...* Sally reminds herself.

As they wait for the memorial to start, Sally looks around and doesn't see anything suspicious. People are quietly whispering to one another, dabbing tissues to their eyes as they remember Gina. Her casket is at the front of the sanctuary, draped with lilies, presumably her favorite flowers. There is a larger-than-life picture of Gina, the same one that was her Facebook profile picture.

The music begins to play, and out of respect, Sally stops scanning the crowd for possible suspects. She pays attention as the family files in. Out of the corner of her eye, she sees movement to her left, and she looks and sees Detective King. They make eye contact, and her stomach rolls. They have seen one another, and his eyes bulge as he sees her as if to say, *What the hell are you doing here?* Sally looks away instinctively.

She keeps her eyes straight ahead throughout the entire memorial and dabs at an involuntary tear here and there. There isn't a dry eye in the house. It's impossible not to notice Gina's parents and siblings sobbing uncontrollably on the front pew. Sally can't imagine how distraught they are and doesn't want to. When the memorial begins to slow, and it is clear it is about to end, Sally leans over to Amanda and tells her they should scoot out early, plus she needs to go to the bathroom.

Following using the restroom, Sally washes her hands as Amanda waits for her outside. The bathroom door swings open, and when Sally looks up, her eyes meet with the bloodshot eyes of Gina's mother. Her breath stops in her chest.

"You. You're Sally Parker, yes?"

"Yes. I am." Sally says in a shaking voice.

"Detective King says you're a suspect, but he recently said he doesn't think you did it. Did you do it? Did you kill my daughter?" Gina's mother seems weary. She has no passion in her voice. Sally can tell she is a shell of her former self, never to be found again. Broken forever.

"I promise you, Mrs. Thorpe, I had nothing to do with it. I found your daughter's purse in the park, and that's how I got involved."

"I could tell by looking at you and being in the same room with you that you didn't do it."

"I'm glad to hear that. And I'm so sorry for your loss," Sally says, and she means it.

"Thank you. But, you know something. Don't you? Tell me."

"What do you m-mean?" Sally asks.

"You know something about what happened to Gina. The police won't tell me anything. Tell me what you know. Right now." She is not aggressive or combative but firm. A mother looking for answers. Much like herself.

"Okay, I did find something. I found a love letter in your daughter's things. And I feel strongly that they are not investigating this to their full potential. That's why I'm involved. Detective King doesn't like that I'm part of this because he thinks I'm trying to point fingers one way or another but I'm not. I'm truly just trying to figure out what happened to your daughter... I'm a mother, too."

"I agree that they are bumbling the investigation, which is a shame. Who was the love letter from?"

"I'm not sure. That's what I'm trying to figure out. That's part of the reason why I came today. Do you have any ideas?"

"I knew she was seeing someone, but I don't know who. I have my suspicions that it was an older man. Because she said that she had to keep it hush-hush. I warned her. I told her not to get involved with a married man. But my Gina was a romantic. She said I didn't understand, but I did, and I do. Now look what happened," she says with a sob.

"Thank you so much for this information. This is truly helpful. I'm still working hard to figure out what happened to your Gina."

"Thank you, dear. Here's my phone number if you hear anything," Mrs. Thorpe scribbled her phone number down on a paper towel as she pulled a pen out of her purse.

They parted ways, and Sally escaped the bathroom. She nearly ran into Amanda and said, "You won't believe who I just talked to in the bathroom- Gina Thorpe's mother."

"What?" Amanda said, eyes widening.

"I know. She asked me if I had killed Gina! She wasn't mean or aggressive at all. She just seemed tired, bless her heart. I feel so bad for her."

"Wow, I did not see that one coming at all," Amanda said.

"I didn't either! But that's not all. She told me that Gina was seeing an older man, possibly an older married man."

"Interesting, but not surprising."

"Agreed. But I can't think of who it would be based on what we know about her. Did you see anything weird in the memorial or anything suspicious?"

"I looked very closely and didn't see anything of note," Amanda said.

"Same. But I did see one person that I had forgotten about... Detective King."

"Oh, crap."

"Oh, crap is right. He made direct eye contact with me and said without using any words that I was in big trouble for being there."

Amanda and Sally got in the car, and Sally began to drive. Before she shifted the car into gear, she looked in the rearview mirror, and at a distance, she saw Detective King standing. Standing silently with his arms crossed, staring. Staring directly at Amanda's car, his gaze unflinching. She knew she was caught in the crosshairs.

"I didn't want to say anything in the parking lot, but I saw King staring right at us." Sally said.

"Us? More like you. He doesn't even know me," Amanda said.

Sally giggled, "Gee, thanks. Good to know you've got my back."

"I do have your back!"

"I know you do."

"So, what are you going to do if and when he calls you out on being there?" Amanda asked.

"I'm not sure. Maybe say I was there to pay my respects? Which would be true. I'm definitely not going to tell him what Mrs. Thorpe told me. He doesn't deserve that information. Although she may have already told him. I don't want to assume I have more information than he does. He definitely has more resources than we do. Still, he doesn't seem to have a care in the world about what actually happened to Gina. And I can't figure out why that is."

"Overworked and underpaid?" Amanda asked.

"That's a good idea and probably a strong contender. But I'm starting to think maybe he doesn't want us to figure out what happened to her."

"You think he might be involved?"

"I'm not saying that. I would never say that," Sally said with a wink. She was still paranoid that she was being watched and listened to.

"Gotcha," Amanda said right as Sally pulled up to her apartment.

Before leaving the apartment complex, Sally wanted to drive by Gina's apartment again. She slowly pulled from one building to the next and finally found the building where Gina made her home and felt safe. Yet she wasn't safe, was she?

Whether her kidnapping happened here or elsewhere, chances are she was being watched and possibly even murdered here. The thought was sickening to Sally. She thought of her own home and how she felt safe. However, since last night her feelings of safety had diminished, walking out the door with William. She wondered if this was the beginning of the end of her marriage, and her throat tensed and eyes prickled.

She didn't want to cry, especially with so much to do. She focused her mind on a man Gina might have fallen into the arms of. A coworker? Her boss? A random guy she met at a bar? Anything was possible. She looked up at Gina's apartment and, for the first time, saw "caution" tape across the door.

Suddenly it dawned on her, Detective King had not even searched Gina's apartment until after Sally did. What a snake... And she began to wonder if Detective King was the one Gina was having an affair with. Or one of his colleagues. Certainly, they would know how to cover up a crime. They would know how to conceal it. They would even know how to point suspicion in another direction. Perhaps even the direction of a woman like herself.

Sally's head was swimming with ideas. Drowning, frankly. She thought Detective King might have actually done this. She drove home so she could use her computer to find more information. She knew Jackson was safe with William and would be fine for a bit more time. She found her computer and opened it.

The record of Gina's address was still on the screen. She deleted Gina's information and input Detective King's. She needed more information. Robert King. Select address. Click.

The webpage loaded more slowly than ever, and wouldn't you know it? Detective King lived in the same apartment complex as Amanda and Gina. Now Sally was sure that King had something to do with it. But she wondered if he was the man Gina was having an affair with or the hitman. Because either could be true.

He was large enough to be able to overpower Gina in a heartbeat. She was so petite, and he was stout and strong, and even though Sally hated to admit it, it was true. She grabbed her phone to text Amanda and momentarily considered how long it had been since she had spoken with Kat. I'll grieve that friendship later, she thought.

Sally: You'll never guess who lives in your apartment complex.

Amanda: Who? The boogeyman?

Sally: Close. Detective King.

Amanda: Shut up.

Sally: I know. Let's discuss later. I've got to get the baby.

Chapter 16

Though her head was swimming with theories of what may have happened: a lover's quarrel, a payout to remove a "problem" for a friend, or an unplanned pregnancy, Sally knew she had to go pick up Jackson. She didn't want him to wear out his welcome at Janie and Bruce's. Although maybe that would be where he was spending time now that William was staying there.

She has no intention of apologizing to William even though she knows that is what she must do to preserve the relationship. It would feel like a step back for her. Sally admits to herself that she has changed but does not wish that she hasn't. She is glad she keeps hanging in there. Used to be a wallflower, codependent, and passive. Now she is the instructor of her own life, and she won't apologize for finding her voice and inner strength. Gina has helped her change; she only wishes she could thank her.

Sally peels herself away from her computer and gets in the car to collect her son. When she arrives, she is nervous because she doesn't want to have a big confrontation with William. Yet, she also doesn't want to pretend like everything is okay between them.

I guess this is what co-parenting is, she thinks. She walks up to the front doors and rings the doorbell. She hears the pitter-patter of little feet, and a smile creeps across her face knowing it must be Jackson. To her surprise, Janice opens the door with Jackson in her arms. They say their "hellos," and Jackson crawls down to go play with his favorite toys here.

"Sally, may I speak with you for a moment?" Janice said.

"Sure," Sally said with trepidation.

"Wonderful. Let's step into the office." Sally followed Janice into Bruce's dark wooden office with touches of leather everywhere. Very manly. Very intimidating.

"Now. I don't know what's going on between the two of you, and I don't need to. But I do need to tell you that a Parker woman does what she must to sustain her marriage. You became a Parker woman once you took those vows. I know it isn't easy. But you must do your diligence to hold your family together."

"Um..." Sally did not know what to say. "All right, Janice. I hear you. But this is none of your business."

"It might surprise you, dear," she said with condescension, "to learn that I, too, had this conversation with the late Mrs. Parker when I was in a state such as yourself. The Parker men are not without their flaws, but it is our duty to keep up appearances."

"Janice., you have no clue what is going on between us, and I won't allow you to speak to me this way."

"Whatever you say, dear." Janice turned on her heel and waltzed out of the office. Sally turned around only to see dark wood everywhere. It was jarring. She could feel her face flushing, and her heart rate was sky-high. Janice was unbelievable. She had no idea what was going on here.

Was she so dim-witted that she couldn't realize that Sally was trying to help someone? Or did she simply not care? She was trying to even the scales of justice. She turned around again and stood face to face with Bruce's desk. It was clean except for one piece of cardstock sticking out from under a fishing magazine. Sally could see a little fleck of gold glimmering from underneath. She slid the paper out from underneath the magazine.

On it a gold-printed bird. The very same bird and the very same stationary that she had found at Gina's apartment. Sally's knees became weak, and she stifled a gasp. Gina was having an affair with Bruce. Her father-in-law. William's father. This changed everything.

Chapter 17

The room began to spin beneath Sally as the realization filled in the room around her. Bruce... Bruce! How can it be Bruce? Bruce was having an affair with Gina. Her own father-in-law. Her mind immediately jumps to William. Poor William.

He knows his parents aren't perfect, but does he know how far from perfect they are? This will be a hard pill to swallow. But should she tell him? This could break him. Of course, she should tell him, but perhaps not now. Things are tense between them already... and what if he doesn't believe her? Surely in his heart, he would know. He must know. But Sally didn't. Could Janice know? She certainly didn't let on, especially with that interesting piece of advice she just imparted on Sally.

The room comes back into focus just as she's about to lose her footing. Her hand reaches out for stability and lands on Bruce's desk, directly on top of the note card. She quickly slides it back underneath the angler magazine. Then she thinks clearly, takes out her phone from the back pocket of her jeans, slides the card out, snaps a picture with her phone, and slides it back... as if she never saw it. She walks out of the office, picks up Jackson, and says a quick goodbye to everyone.

When she arrives home, it is bedtime for Jackson. She quickly does the bedtime routine, something she used to delight in and now something that she checks off her list. Feelings of guild suppressed under the anxiety about her earlier discovery. Following bedtime, she calls Amanda.

"Hello?" she answers.

"Hey. I have a lead. A really good one, at that. Can you come over?"

"Sure. When?"

"Now."

"I'll be right there," Amanda says.

"Great, I'll text you my address," Sally says. This is the first time Amanda will come to Sally's home, and she's nervous. She hopes her home isn't too stuffy for Amanda.

She slides around the living room, picking up Jackson's toys and doing a few dishes while she anxiously awaits Amanda's arrival. She sees Amanda's headlights and walks to the front door before she gets a chance to knock. She opens the door to see Amanda's large brown eyes.

"Come in," Sally says. "You won't believe what I'm about to tell you."

"Tell me!" Amanda practically shouts.

"Shhh! The baby's asleep."

"Oh, sorry," she says now in the faintest whisper. There is no in-between for Amanda. Sally reaches for her phone and finds the picture of the stationary.

"Here. Look. The exact match for the stationary I found at Gina's."

"Oh my God," Amanda gasps. "Where did you find this?"

"My father-in-law's desk. Hidden under a magazine."

"Shut your freaking mouth." Amanda seems as stunned as Sally was to find it.

"I know. I was shocked too. Still am," Sally says. "But what do I do now?"

"We've got to find proof that they were a couple," Amanda says.

"But how?"

"I'll handle that part," Amanda says.

Amanda grabs her phone and opens Instagram. She searches for Gina's Instagram and scrolls through all of her photos, then moves along to tagged posts. Nothing incriminating there. No proof of a relationship. No sign of Bruce at all. "What's your father-in-law's name?" Amanda asks.

"Bruce," Sally says.

"I'm on it."

"Exactly what are you looking for?" Sally asks.

"I think there's a good chance she has a finsta."

"A finsta? What is that?"

"A fake Instagram account. She has one for the public and one for herself." Amanda searches for accounts similar to Gina's main account. "Do you have a picture of Bruce?"

"I'm sure I do. Let me look," Sally said as she scrolled through her phone. There were so few pictures of Bruce, but she finally found one. Jackson with his grandparents on Christmas morning. She cropped the photo so only his face shone. "Here's one."

"Send it to me," Amanda said. Sally airdropped the photo to Amanda's phone. "Found it. I did a special Google search using several filters. @inlovewithbruce it is. Come take a look."

Together they poured over the photographs. It seems there are endless pictures of Gina and Bruce together. Pictures of them kissing, pictures of them in the car together, of him kissing her, of her kissing him, of them on vacation together.

Why in the world was she interested in him? It seems incredibly unlikely that the two of them would fall in love, but the proof is right before their eyes. Bruce's short gray hair, next to Gina's bright blonde hair, looks almost like a father and daughter... or grandfather and granddaughter. A shiver goes from the top of her head down her spine.

But if they were so in love, then why would Bruce kill her? Perhaps he was in danger of Janice finding out. That would make Sally fearful as well. Janice was no one to trifle with. William once called her "mean as a snake," and she knew that she was. Bruce did seem fearful of her at times, but it also seemed as if he hid things from her rather than have a confrontation with Janice.

He always swore up and down that he didn't smoke cigars, but everyone knew he did. But no one knew about this. At least to Sally's knowledge.

"So, what do we do now?" Sally asked.

"That's your call. He's your father-in-law. Do you think he did it?"

"I have never seen him violent, but I don't know how it couldn't have been him. All the signs are there."

"I agree. I think he did it. But I also don't think you should tell Detective King."

"You don't? This could be the smoking gun to get me off the hook."

"He would say that you planted it."

"I didn't think about that," Sally said, "you're probably right. He doesn't believe a word I say."

"Because he thinks you're guilty."

"I know. I'm debating whether to tell William or not. I'll try to smooth things out with him before I hit him with this bomb."

"Let me know when you do so I can find a bomb shelter with plenty of canned beans," Amanda jokes.

Chapter 18

Over the next week, things with William seem to improve. They are speaking more often, never about Gina. She knows not to bring it up to him yet. She needs to get him back home first. Sally continues to wonder what the right move for their family is.

No matter how she packages the information, this will make their family system crumble. She must find a gentle way to tell William. But how do you tell someone that their father is a killer and a cheater? That he has been lying for months if not years? That your parents' marriage is all a lie?

The weight of it all is too much to bear for Sally alone. She is thankful she has an outlet in Amanda. Their friendship has grown, and sometimes she feels consumed by what she must tell Amanda and when. Amanda is endlessly patient with Sally and gives her advice when she asks and a listening ear when she doesn't. They both wonder how to get the police involved when Detective

King is so short-sided and single-minded when it comes to this case.

One Wednesday afternoon, while Sally is giving Jackson a bath, it comes to her. A bubble pops in Jackson's bath, and at that exact moment, a lightbulb goes off in Sally's head: Gina was pregnant. It is the only logical explanation. She has never seen Bruce reactive or aggressive in any way. In fact, she has never even seen him argue with anyone. It is so unusual to her that he could become so ferocious as to take a human life.

This is the only reason- his entire life at stake. Everything to lose. He's an older man, a baby surely would not be welcome. And oh, the reaction from Janice. The thought is enough to terrify a wolf. But again, there is no proof. However, this hasn't been a long-term issue for Sally. She has always found it; it is just a matter of time.

Sally tries to spend as much time at Janice and Bruce's home as possible. Even though she is fearful, she tries to gather intelligence whenever she is in their presence. She doesn't mention Gina explicitly, but she mentions things that might make them spill information accidentally, especially Janice.

Janice loves to hear her own voice and thinks everything she says is of utmost importance. She tells William that she thinks Jason is having an affair, and Katherine doesn't know what to do. Janice and Bruce are both in the room when she says it, and she watches each of their reactions like a hawk. Bruce doesn't even blink or look up from his magazine- does he even know Gina is dead? Janice says under her breath, "She should kill him."

Sally thinks back to her own childhood and the marriage between her parents. Different from Bruce and Janice, yet the same in many ways. Their generation is known for not speaking about conflict directly. Why have an uncomfortable discussion when you can sweep it under the rug?

Sure, it festers, but at least you don't have to confront it directly. Sally's parents may have handled difficult situations behind closed doors, but the resentment she saw and felt daily suggested otherwise. They were the typical American family; dad goes off to work all day while mom stays home with the kids.

Sally thought this was the life that she, too, wanted. But now she is beginning to question it. Did she want it because it was what was designed for her, or was it what she really wanted? Through the investigation with Gina, she was starting to find an answer. She wanted her own life, her own independence, apart from being a mother.

Thursday came, and Jackson went to school. Sally called William and asked him to have lunch. They were taking steps toward reconciliation, but Sally had to act as if she was no longer interested in what happened with Gina.

She thought about what that might mean for their relationship, hiding who she was and what she really wanted. But she wasn't willing to consider divorce. At least not yet. Their lunchtime conversation was very vanilla, very surface-level. Again, Sally wondered if this was what she wanted. Did she want to spend the rest of her life pretending to be happy or actually be happy? She pushed the thought down. She had to figure out what happened to Gina first.

Sally called Amanda. "Hello?" Amanda answered.

"Hey. I'm starting to have doubts that Bruce did this. He's showing absolutely no indication of guilt. So, either he's a total sociopath, or he really didn't do this."

"But isn't it also strange that he isn't even showing a whisper of despair when his 'love' died?" Amanda asked.

"Completely weird. I also wonder who he confides in, if anyone."

"Does he have a laptop we can swipe and look at?" Amanda asks.

"Not that I know of, but I can sneak around and look the next time I'm at their house," Sally says.

"Do that, and we'll go from there."

Chapter 19

Sally's phone rings at five a.m. It's William. "William?" she answers and asks.

"My dad's in jail."

"What do you mean he's in jail?"

"I know it's insane. Can I come over? I'll explain everything."

"Of course you can, William. This is your home too."

William races to their home and is there in record time. Jackson is still asleep, so they have time to talk. He walks in the door, and they kiss. Their first kiss since he left. It feels so good, so right, so comfortable that Sally gets lost in it. William pulls away, ready to give Sally all the information to the questions she has already forgotten about.

"My dad got in a car accident driving late at night. I have no idea what he was doing driving on the interstate at two in the morning, but he was. When the police came, they found that there was an outstanding warrant for his arrest."

"For what?" Sally asks.

"Unpaid child support," William says.

"What?" Sally asks. She can't compute what William is saying. She looks up, and William's head is in his hands.

"I can't believe I have to clean up this mess. Apparently, years ago, my father had an affair which resulted in a child. He told me all of this on the phone when he asked me to bail him out. And he never paid the child support the woman requested."

"Oh, William. I'm so sorry." Sally reaches for William. She wants to take him in her arms and tell him it will all be alright. But she knows she can't do that. Because that would be a lie. She knows now is not the time to tell him that his father has possibly and probably killed a separate woman that he was having an affair with. This is all too much information for one day, she decides.

"I'm going to go get my dad out of jail at seven this morning," William says.

"Do you want me to come with you?" Sally asks.

"No, you don't need to do that. But you might want to go keep my mom company. She is completely wrecked over this whole thing, as you can imagine. Not the information someone would like to hear after forty years of marriage in the middle of the night."

"Of course. I'll do whatever you need," Sally says.

When Jackson wakes up, Sally does their morning routine that they both know well. She takes her time getting ready to go to Janice's because, well, she doesn't want to. She doesn't know what to say or do in the face of this overwhelming turmoil. What do you say when someone's life comes crashing down? Sally doesn't know, but she will try her best to summon all the empathy, and acting skills, in her body.

Sally drives slowly to Janice's home. She is trying to stay away as long as she can but knows she must go. Go to the crisis. She feels nearly unable to go, but she knows she must. It is her duty. In sickness and in health. The vows she took: sickness. This is a sickness, but not the sickness she predicted.

She always thought those vows meant physical sickness. But here she was, dealing with a generational sickness. A psychological sickness. A sickness of the mind that permeates through the whole family. Bruce had no idea that the consequences of his actions were a ripple effect and touched everyone in the family. His selfish decisions showed that he cared for no one but himself.
She pulled into the driveway of their stately home, and everything looked the same, normal. But it is anything but normal. She walks to the door and gingerly knocks, and the door opens slightly. Must not have been totally shut, she thinks. Sally walks inside carrying Jackson.

There is an eerie feeling inside the home, but Sally pushes past it like she is walking through a cloud of smoke. She dismisses it as awkwardness from the current situation. She walks around the house looking for Janice, calling for her. She knows it is early, but certainly, Janice is awake, given the circumstances.

Finally, she finds Janice sitting in Bruce's dark office in his desk chair. She is looking at papers strewn about his desk, evidently something she has done because this is not how Bruce keeps his office. "Janice, hi," Sally says quietly, "how are you?"

"Not well. Not well at all."

"I know this is hard," Sally says in her most compassionate tone. Sure, she and Janice have not always seen eye-to-eye on everything, but this is something no wife, no mother, no person ever wants to go through. Especially not alone.

"You have absolutely no idea," Janice says in a hard and severe tone. "I should have killed him when I had the chance."

Sally was looking down, but she looks up and sees the darkness in Janice. The room fills with anger seeping from Janice, and Sally feels her stomach fill with fear. She realizes in this moment; this isn't just about Bruce. This is about Gina. Janice is dangerous.

"Janice, I'm so sorry this is happening," Sally tries to keep her tone even though she is fearful. She takes one step backward. She is holding Jackson and must protect him, even from the feelings pouring out of Janice.

"This isn't the first time this has happened, you know," Janice looks at Sally, and their eyes meet. "He's been doing this for years. I've always known. He thinks I'm stupid, but I'm not. I'm a hell of a lot smarter than him. He thinks I just sit at home and twiddle my thumbs. But I don't. I'm the proactive one."

"Janice, can I ask you something?" She knows this is her chance. This is her one shot. Janice has let her guard down and is possibly on the edge of a psychotic break, so she must move swiftly.

"Why not?" Janice says with a guffaw.

"Did you know about Gina?"

"Of course I did! Don't be ridiculous."

"Janice, did you kill Gina Thorpe?"

"It's not as simple as that," Janice says.

"What do you mean?" Sally says, her breath catching in her throat. It sounds like she is going to cry, but that is not what is going on. She is afraid, deeply and profoundly afraid. She wants to keep Janice talking, but she also must keep her son safe. She slowly backs away as she continues to ask questions.

"I told you to stop digging, Sally. Why wouldn't you just leave it alone? We could have made it out of this easily. But you couldn't leave well enough alone." Janice stood up and in the corner, Sally could see the glint of metal in her hand. Bruce's letter opener.

"You did it, Janice, you killed her."

Before she knew what happened, Janice lunged toward Sally with the letter opener. Sally stepped back, so Janice narrowly missed her with the letter opener. She turned and ran. Everything is a blur. She can't see colors.

She only sees herself running, clutching her small son to her chest. She sees herself as if she is floating above herself, watching. None of this feels real. All that she hears in her head is her own blood pumping and the sound of her own voice telling her to run.

She turns the corner to the front door. She hears footsteps behind her, getting closer, closer, closer. She sees her car in front of her. She only prays she can make it. Jackson begins to cry in her arms. She cannot soothe him, only protect him.

Keep him alive. Keep yourself alive. Don't let her catch you. She hears a loud thud behind her. She doesn't look back; she only keeps running. What was that, she wonders. Did Janice throw something at her? Was it a gunshot? It didn't sound like a gunshot, but she does not know what it would sound like so close to you. So near to you. It might sound like a bomb, and it might sound like a clap, she has no idea. The brain might make it sound different to protect the mind and the memory.

She reaches the front door and pulls. Almost there, she thinks, almost to safety. Don't let go of the baby. She clutches him to her chest, her fingernails nearly digging into him. He squeals out in pain as she pulls him closer. She gets out the door and to the car. She yanks open the car door and throws Jackson into the passenger seat.

No time to put him in his car seat, she thinks. She starts the car, and the engine roars to life. She locks the doors and takes a breath. She only now realizes that she is wet. It is raining. Pouring. How fitting, she thinks. My life falls apart, and the sky falls as well. She looks to the front door, standing wide open, and doesn't see Janice. She puts the car in drive and pulls out of the driveway as quickly as possible.

Sally looks over to Jackson, and she sees fear in his wet eyes. He is crying in fear and confusion. She reaches for him and puts him in her lap as she drives. "It's going to be alright, precious one," she tells not only him but herself as well. She looks down and sees the imprint of her fingernails on his chubby thighs. But she releases the air from her lungs in the form of a sigh and tells herself, you kept him safe. You're alive, and so is he. You are safe.

Sally pulls into her own driveway and feels safe but not safety. She won't feel completely safe until William is with her. She takes Jackson inside and rocks him, calming him with sweet songs that make him feel safe. You are my sunshine, she sings. He falls asleep on her chest, and she rocks him a while longer until she feels secure he is sleeping, gently placing him in his crib. His own sense of protection.

She sneaks out of his room, arms, and legs shaking, and runs to her phone to call William. He answers on the first ring.

"William, your mother tried to kill me." She says bluntly. Because that is what happened. There is no other way to put it.

"What!" he nearly shouts into the phone.

"Abandon your father and come home. Your family needs you. Your real family."

"I'm coming," he says with conviction.

Chapter 20

William runs to her as he enters the doors. Sally is magnetic and their hearts reach for one another. They can only hug. They cannot speak. There are no words now. Only safety and space between them.

"What happened?" William gently asks. Sally begins to cry and realizes this is the first time she has cried since Janice attacked her.

"William, I think your mother killed Gina Thorpe. In fact, I know she did. She all but admitted it to me and then attacked me with a letter opener. Jackson and I narrowly got away."

"Good God. I don't know what to say." It is clear he believes her. She was so worried he wouldn't.

"I don't know where she is now," Sally says.

"I'll find her," William answers. He walks to the door and shuts it behind him. Fear fills Sally's every extremity as she realizes she is completely and utterly alone in their home. Janice could come back and try to harm them again.

Fear is consuming, and she feels like an animal being hunted, constantly keeping her eyes wide open and looking left to right, then behind her, always watching, always wondering where someone could be hiding. She does this paranoid dance for nearly three hours until William returns. He walks through the door, his eyes red and swollen.

"My mother is dead, Sally." He says. His eyes fill with tears. "She's dead," and a sob escapes his mouth. Sally runs to him and hugs him, the sobs escaping from her body as well. Hers are not like his, though. His are sobs of grief, of a little boy losing his mother. Hers are from relief. Safety.

"You were right, Sally. You were right about everything."

"Shhhh," she tells him. She knows they will get all of the answers they never wanted later.

Evening comes, and Sally and William find themselves staring blankly. They are living in a state of shock at what has become of their family. Once a family that was a pillar of strength and of their community, now they hide inside their home with the curtains drawn. Word has not even reached society, where it will spread like an unwelcome weed, no spade unable to stop it.

There is a knock at their door, and William and Sally immediately look at one another. They look so quickly it is almost as if they jump, and perhaps they do. Sally stands first and nods to William as if to say, I've got this. And she walks to the door. Her feet feel as if they're in mud, she pulls them up, and yet they still sink and stick to the floor. Grief and fear pull her down like gravity. She finally reaches the door after what feels like years, but it was only moments. She pulls open the door, and before her stands Detective King. She is stunned.

"May I come in?" he asks sheepishly. Sally doesn't answer with words but instead pulls the door open farther and steps back. She feels like she is all out of words after today. She keeps them locked away in a safe for only those who are most precious to her; William and Jackson.

Detective King moves to sit next to William. "I am so sorry for your loss," he says so quietly it is almost imperceptible.

"Thank you," William says, but he doesn't mean it.

"It seems as if your mother was the perpetrator after all," Detective King says. "We found a note that she wrote. It does seem as if her death was an accident. She fell when she was allegedly chasing Sally and hit her head on the corner of the desk." Sally bristles at the word allegedly and feels as if King is making a dig at her.

He continues, "The note laid out everything we needed to know. Apparently, Gina Thorpe was pregnant, and Janice made a plan to meet her under the guise of being Bruce. According to the note, she was not planning on killing Gina, but things got heated, and one thing led to another. We see this a lot. Crimes of passion. Gina never stood a chance." Sally and William both grimace at his last statement.

"Can we see the note?" William asks.

"Since the perpetrator is now deceased, this is a closed case. I have some paperwork to do to tie up loose ends, but after that, I will give you the note." Detective King uses words like "perpetrator" and "deceased" and Sally thinks that sensitivity training might serve him well. He gets up to leave, and William speaks.

"Detective King," he asks, "do you have anything you'd like to say to my wife?" He sounds almost as if he is speaking to a child. *What do you say?*

"My apologies for assuming you were involved, Mrs. Parker," he says sheepishly.

"Apology accepted," Sally says. She doesn't mean it. Not in the slightest. She hates him. He makes her blood boil. But she wants him out of her house forever, and this is the quickest way to get him out. He lets himself out, and Sally looks to William. "What about your dad?" she asks. He lets out a groan as if to say, I forgot.

"I'll deal with him later," he says. "We both need sleep." They both wander to the bedroom like zombies and fall into bed without even changing clothes. Dreamless sleep gracefully finds them quickly.

William and Sally wake to the morning light peeking through the curtains and the sound of Jackson singing in his crib. They open their eyes at the same time and Sally can see reality slip into William's mind's eye. He suddenly remembers all that happened yesterday. His family falling apart. His mother's death. His father in jail. He wipes his hand over his face. It doesn't help.

"Morning," Sally says, purposefully leaving out "good."

"Hi," William says.

"What's the plan?" Sally asks. She ponders if this is the right time. Too much too soon, perhaps? But there is no use in pretending what happened has not. It is their reality, and they may as well confront it head-on. Sally thinks about the family culture of the Parkers. She wants to change it. Change it all. Starting today. She won't mention this to William just yet.

He has a lot of grieving and processing to do. Sally does as well, much less than William. She is sure he is questioning what is real and what isn't. What was real about his childhood, and what wasn't. Surely, he is reeling from it all. Processing. Traumatized. Sally certainly is, and it isn't even her parents.

William speaks softly. "I think I'm going to let my father clean up his own mess."

"I support you," Sally says.

Chapter 21

Following the unraveling of the Parker family, Sally and William tried to hide. But they couldn't. When the news broke of Janice's involvement in Gina Thorpe's murder, the media had an absolute field day.

They camped out on Sally and William's lawn, knocked on their front door, followed their cars, the works. They could run, but they couldn't hide. You can only say "no comment" so many times before it begins to crack your psyche.

Amanda and Katherine kept Sally abreast of the news stories that came out about Janice and Gina, but only the ones she needed to know about. They would give her the CliffsNotes, here's what they said, here's what's true, here's what isn't. Some of the stories were so incorrect they were almost laughable. Almost. But it isn't funny when it's your life. There would be podcasts and books. She knew that. She wished she had never listened to a single true crime podcast.

They felt they were being watched everywhere they went. Sally and William could handle it somewhat, and they feared for Jackson's safety. They wanted to shield him from whatever they could. They decided it would be in the best interest of their family to move.

They moved to Lake Littlejohn, ironically the last place Gina used her credit card. The ghost of Gina would follow them forever. But they found a cabin on the lake that was perfect for their family, and Jackson loved to throw rocks in the lake and swim. They continued their life together anew.

As Jackson took his afternoon nap, Sally walked down to the lake. She rediscovered her peace there. She processed her trauma there. She and William were able to talk openly and freely there, without the chains of society pulling them into a mold of perfection. Sally was able to tell William what she wanted, what she really wanted out of her life, and he listened and accepted her.

She wanted more. She started her own billing company. She was able to send Jackson to preschool and work from home. She picked him up from school and worked while he was at school. The beauty of owning your own business, she would often tell herself as she drove to pick him up. As she walked to the lake on this specific day, she rubbed her growing belly. The newest addition to the family that they were building from the ground up. They were starting over.

Sally and William felt the undercurrent that people knew what had happened with their family, their former family, but it seemed as if no one cared. They made new friends but kept them at arm's length. They were still processing and protecting themselves from more hurt.

Bruce was still in jail and was ordered to serve one year for his unpaid child support. William no longer answered his phone calls, and they spoke of him rarely. They had a small graveside funeral for Janice before they moved. Family only. The media tried to gain access, but the cemetery and funeral home were good about helping them keep them away. With any luck, Jackson wouldn't remember them at all.

They would be honest with him and tell him everything when it was age appropriate. They had begun working to change the family culture. William struggled with openness and communication, but that was a "make it or break it" for Sally, and he agreed to try his best.
They hadn't heard from Detective King since he came to their house on the day of Janice's death. They had all but forgotten about the turmoil that he had subjected them to, namely Sally.

One fall afternoon, she was checking the mail and found an overstuffed envelope with Detective King's professional return address. Her stomach lurched at the sight of his name. She took it inside and opened it. She still couldn't bring herself to use a letter opener after Janice had attacked her with one. In fact, she threw away their letter opener in the move.

The irony was that Janice had gifted her with that very letter opener as a post-wedding gift. "Every lady has a letter opener," she had said. The words echoed in her mind as she watched it fall, silver and sharp, into the bottom of the trash bin.

Sally pulled the items from the bubble mailer and was surprised at what she found. Janice's favorite Rolex watch, dainty and a mix of silver and gold, that she wore daily. Sally was surprised the police had possession of it and not the funeral home.

She wondered about the protocol for who got what items. She pictured them taking turns grabbing items off and around her body. "You get this one, I get this one," she pictured them to say. Taking turns like children.

Seeing Janice's watch brought a flood of memories. She wondered if it would be fruitful to share these things with William or if it would only further this pain. But she knew she had to. Following her very own lead, she had to be open and honest with him. She could not expect these things from him and not offer them herself.

Next, she felt in the mailer and felt cold, hard metal. She knew before she removed it that it was the letter opener. She dropped it on the cold tile floor, and the sound of metal on tile reverberated throughout their entire home. She was instantly transported into the moment when Janice was chasing her, and she clutched tight to Jackson, willing herself to survive if only to shield him. Not just a mother's love but a mother's protection.

Next out of the package came a scarf, which was inconsequential to Sally. Finally, there was an envelope. On the outside of the envelope said, "For William," in Janice's shaky handwriting. She would have known it anywhere.

Sally called William. "Hello?" he answered.

"We just got a package."

"Okay," he was confused, "what kind?"

"From Detective King," she elaborated, "your mother's things."

"I'll be home as fast as I can."

Living in a small community had so many positives, but one of the big ones for Sally was being able to drive from one side of town to the other in just ten minutes. She knew William would be home quickly. He walked through the door seven minutes after their conversation had ended.

"What's in the package?" he asked without saying hello.

"Here," she said and showed him everything as she had laid it out on the counter. His hands gently touched the watch, almost as if it would emit an electric spark if he touched it too hard or too quickly.

He picked up the scarf in both hands and brought it to his face, and inhaled. He was smelling it. His eyes focused back to reality, and he looked to Sally, embarrassed. She gave his hand a gentle squeeze to say, whatever you need to do, no judgment from me. Finally, he saw the letter opener on the floor, she gently moved it with her foot so he would notice.

He picked it up and looked to her. "Yes," she said, answering his question without him uttering a word. Sadness filled his eyes. Regret that he had put his wife and child in such a dangerous situation.

He had tearfully shared his feelings of remorse and asked Sally for forgiveness for asking them to go be with his mother. Sally didn't have an ounce of anger toward him, only Janice. But she knew he still felt repentance.

She pushed the letter towards him, and he touched it gently. He turned it over and opened it. As he read the words, she watched his eyes and his face. She saw one emotion after another come over him.

The emotions she was seeing looked to be anger, sadness, embarrassment, and regret. She thought once again that he was not responsible for the sins of his father and mother. When he had finished reading, he pushed the letter to Sally, and she began to read.

My dearest William,

You won't see me again, my darling. I'm going to go away. Far away, where no one will find me. Not even God because I can't answer for what I've done. Perhaps I should start from the beginning.

Now is the time for me to finally be honest with you about what has happened. I was young, so very young, when I married your father. I was poor, William. I had no money. I was afraid. I was a housekeeper, and he showed interest in me. He asked me on a date, and I said yes. I kept saying yes to whatever he asked me. And that became the layout of our relationship. He asked something of me, and I said yes. Always yes.

I know people will think me a monster, but I am not. I promise you I am not. I did all of this to protect you, to protect our family. I didn't want it to unravel as it has today. I cry as I write these words. Your father is a good man with oftentimes bad behavior. I have always been able to separate the two.

His first affair was when we had been married for not even a year. He always thought himself a sneak. An undercover agent of sorts. He thought he hid it all so well. But I always knew. They say a woman always knows. That isn't eternally true. I had friends who didn't know. They were so dim that they were clueless.

But me, I always knew. I never confronted him until I suspected a pregnancy or a child. That was twenty years ago. What your father is now in jail for. What a fool. I now know what I should have done was partner with the women he was sleeping with and work together to end him. I see where my mistakes lie now.

I supposed now I must confess about Gina. I found his notes to her. Your father is so old-fashioned. I admit I do love that about him. You might wonder how I can still love him. Well, love and hate can coexist. In fact, they are not so different at all. They are much the same. I found his letters to her and hers to him.

I wrote one pretending to be him. I wanted to meet with her and tell her to move along. There had been plenty like her, and my patience was running thin. I am an old woman, and I no longer have tolerance for frivolity.

Except I underestimated her. God bless her soul; she was a feisty one. That is most likely what he loved about her. When she realized who I was, she said she wouldn't go down without a fight. I quickly saw that she meant what she said. I told her to leave our family alone, and that's when she dropped the bomb. She was pregnant. Not just pregnant. But pregnant with twins.

I hate that you have to find out this way, William. But I am so ashamed that I can't look you in the eyes. I was blind with rage. I thought about you and Sally and baby Jackson. I couldn't bear for you to have a brother or sister, or both, the same age as your own child. How disgusting. She was spitting mad and said he was going to leave me. I laughed and turned to leave. She grabbed me by the shoulder and spun me around, nearly knocking me off balance. I know I shouldn't speak ill of the dead, but she was quite rude considering the circumstances. You would think she would be more kind to the woman whose husband she was having an affair with. Unfortunately, not.

Well, William, when she touched me like that, I only saw the color red. I have heard it said before that someone saw red when angry. I had never experienced it until that moment, and I saw the red. It was fascinating. I didn't realize what was happening until it was over. I went and grabbed that little pistol out of my glovebox that your father gave me in case I was carjacked. Oh, the irony. And I shot right at her. I missed the first time, and she screamed.

Thankfully we had met in the woods. This is where Sally found her purse. What a dull woman. She probably thought it romantic of him. Luckily no one was around, and no one heard those two gunshots, to my knowledge. I want you to know, William, she didn't suffer. She was gone very quickly.

After I realized what I had done, I panicked. I summoned all of my strength and moved her body to the trunk of my car. I know you might think me frail, William, but I did it all alone. Can you believe it? I waited until the cover of the night and pushed her body off a bridge I had never noticed before. It had low railings. It was quite difficult to push her up and over, but again, I did it all myself. Your father didn't even notice I was gone.

I would have gotten away with it, and all would have been fine if Sally hadn't poked around so much. You really should learn to get a handle on her, William. She is out of control.

When she went missing, your father carved up his acting chops and didn't act interested. He still doesn't know that I did it. I'll never tell him, just like he never admitted to having an affair. I asked him time and time again; he never would be forthcoming. If you feel so inclined, help your father with his legal battles. I simply do not care, but you may. I give you my blessing to help him if you see fit.

I am thinking about what other information you might want or need to move on with your life. I have always loved you, my darling. No one as much as you. You are the greatest gift your father ever gave me, and I am eternally grateful for that. That is why I killed Gina and not him. Because he gave me you, and I didn't want to hurt you. I love you.

Mother

There was a note stuck to the bottom of the letter. It read, "Wanted you to know. We did an autopsy. Gina wasn't pregnant." It was signed, "Detective King."

The End

Feedback Request

I would love and appreciate it if you could leave a review. I love bringing stories to life and your feedback helps to keep me going.

Thank you for reading.

[Leave a review here.](#)